Like Father Like Son

Idle Hands, book 1

Michael B. Chikondi

To Melanie, my editor, whom I love (or who?)

To my dear spouse for endless proofreading, and endlessly answering the questions: 'But is my writing bad, though? Are you sure? You'd definitely tell me?'

And my little child, for being cute.

Contents

Prologue

S injen stood, feet bare, on the sand of Whitby beach. The gaslights and windows of the town cast a sparkling reflection over the calm, dark waters of the North Sea. He pushed a thick strand of slimy kelp aside with his foot, the beach stinking of oil and decaying seaweed so close to the tideline. It was close to midnight, just an hour left. Did he really want to see another year?

A wave broke over his feet, only gentle but the biting cold saltwater stung on contact. Yet another reminder of what he was. He *could* walk in, a few more steps wouldn't be too difficult. He'd never really learnt to swim, but much beyond a paddle shouldn't be needed. When it hurt too much, he could go into torpor. The tide, he hoped, would carry him away, and then what would happen? Underwater, the sun shouldn't wake him or burn him. He'd be left to the fish and crabs, unless he washed ashore, but if he did, he'd die in agony.

He sighed. This wasn't the way to do it. He should have brought something heavy and rented a boat. He would have, if he'd been serious.

1

He'd skipped his own party, though he had another tomorrow night. Eliza wouldn't care anyway. He'd made sure Lord Marlais was with her, and they'd be amused with one another, as always. It was the first New Year's Eve she'd ever let him be alone for. Perhaps that was a good sign, but he suspected she'd make him pay for it. He checked his pocket watch. Forty minutes till he had to face his fifty-first year after death.

No, this was enough morbidity, he hadn't endured everything else to give up while his enemies still lived. Marlais and Eliza would die before he did, or he'd have amounted to nothing. Half a century of torment deserved a whiskey, even if he was six months belated. How could he have forgotten until now? He picked up a cuttlefish bone for Carlotta's budgie, 'Major Key,' the little blue bastard.

Retrieving his shoes, he wandered towards the changing huts and slipped between two to fully dress again. 'How could I risk a young lady seeing an unclothed foot?' he thought, smiling to himself. At least he could pretend to be respectable amongst normal society. There should be fireworks, and new friends to make tonight.

New Year, New Friends

Chapter 1

New Year might be the best night there was: nobody was asleep and everyone was careless. The streets were filled with people, all heading to get a good view of the fireworks display. They'd be on the harbour, perhaps also at the Abbey. A good-looking man staggered past him, then tapped his shoulder, causing him to turn.

"Man like you, on your own?" he said, grinning. Sinjen had noticed him at once, for his figure and red hair, but his dark blue eyes shone with a compelling intensity.

"I'm afraid so," Sinjen replied, taking a closer look at him. He'd dressed up, and must have had enough to spend, but his style showed a deliberate disregard for order and convention. It was rather charming.

"Come meet my mates." He gestured toward a spot which was not too busy, higher up than where Sinjen would have chosen. It should have a

3

decent view. "We're gonna watch the fireworks together, then go back to the pub."

Sinjen smiled. He could recognise the danger but went anyway.

"You got family?" the young man asked. "I'm Jack, by the way."

"Looks like you've already had a few tonight, Jack. No, my family has passed."

"No wife?" he said, looking Sinjen up and down. He shook his head. "And you such a looker. Never mind, I heard there are some fine mermaids, over there, see?" He took Sinjen's elbow, and pointed down the coast. Sinjen almost laughed, and casually flicked Jack's hand away from his pocket. Jack turned to him, smiled a charming smile and winked. Sinjen chuckled, and allowed Jack to put his arm around his shoulder.

They met his friends, Larry and Archie, and watched the fireworks. A meagre display compared to one of his own. Next year, screw it, he'd donate some to the town.

"Sound like cannons," Archie said. All were at least a bit tipsy.

"My dog bloody hates 'em. Should be illegal," Tom complained, "but I heard they have huge shows in London."

"My dad went once. He skated on the Thames," Sinjen volunteered.

"You bloody liar," Jack laughed, smacking him on the shoulder, "That hasn't happened since my great-grandad's day."

Sinjen laughed, "Alright, you got me."

"Ah, come on," Archie said, grinning, "let's go get lush."

When they were all together in the pub, and had drunk a great deal more, Tom turned to Jack. "Look at him, his face. How's 'e standin' up?"

"I'm afraid you might all be lightweights," Sinjen said with a small smile. Jack hadn't managed to pick his pocket. He wasn't trying not to get caught at this point either, just letting Sinjen pinch him when he tried.

"Oi, no, never!" Jack laughed. "Big Dave!"

A burly man came out from behind the bar. "What is it, guv?"

"This one's not going down, come fix it for us."

"Aye, but you're paying the tab," Dave said, pulling two bottles of whiskey and two half-pint glasses from behind the bar.

"Oh my, you three aren't playing around," Sinjen said, amused.

"You bet," Dave said, with a loud laugh. "The game is simple, we drink till one of us can't no more. You can give up, or you can die. I don't care either way."

"Well, that sounds easy enough," Sinjen said, and poured a full glass of whiskey for both of them.

By two-thirty in the morning, Dave was still glaring at him, but having to hold onto the table to stay above it. Sinjen was rather tipsy, but he'd been playing up his drunkenness for effect. A small crowd had gathered, and begun placing bets on who would remain.

"Last one. Last!" Jack called to the bar in general. "If they both survive it, then we call it a tie. Alright?" he nodded to the bartender.

"You're on," Sinjen grinned, feeling content.

"Yeh?" Dave growled. "Let's go."

"A battle of bricks," Tom laughed as Jack filled their drinks.

"The kind of men our England's made of," Archie declared, more than a little intoxicated himself. He was resting his head on his hand, an elbow on the table and smiling widely at everyone, having lost the ability to focus on anyone in particular.

Sinjen watched Dave down his drink, but gave up when he thought he'd reached his limit. It wouldn't be fair to let the poor man actually die. "I can't go on any more, but I'll pay the bill." He handed the drink back to Jack.

"Ah, you're funny, mate. Next time you're in Whitby come see us again," Jack said, patting his back.

"Oh? So you can try and rob me again? Where would I have ended up?"

"Ah, on the beach probably, but you'd have been alright." Jack laughed. "Hey, come see my sister tonight. We'll get your money off you between us, I don't doubt."

"Well, I won't spoil your fun," Sinjen agreed, and let Jack drag him away after he'd paid up.

It was a dirty backstreet, but somehow feminine. A dead end, surrounded by squat apartments, each overlooking the secluded road. The main building before them, brick like the others, was better lit, and they could hear voices and music from within, echoing throughout the little cul-de-sac. He looked around, Jack still at his side. "Why does this seem..."

"Womanly?" Jack laughed. "It's all the flowers in the windows. The laundry drying, even at night, and the stale perfume. Don't worry, it's what everyone says."

"And these women are?"

"Yeah, all are of negotiable virtue. My sister runs it. Don't tell anyone, but I helped her get rid of the last owner, a huge man, a real beast to the girls. But here, your heart's desire can always be bought for the right price. Want a mistress? A princess? A set of triplets? An artist, or great wit, even just a simple girl? If they don't have what you want, my Caroline will find her for you. Few in England, perhaps the world, have her skill and acumen.

"This here, however it looks from outside, is a palace of lust. Your desire is their pleasure, and your pleasure is their desire and trade, but you always get what you pay for, so pay well."

Sinjen raised an eyebrow. "Which one is your sister?"

"Oi! Carol!" he called, and a few laughs came from the windows.

"Oh, Jack!" a pretty voice called. They saw a delicate face appear from a window and break into a wide smile. "Have you come back for me?"

"Ah, I'll never stop coming back, even when you're old and crusty and I'm a bag of bones!" he said, his laugh echoing through the dank brick alley.

A few girls came out and peered down at them from behind the railings, each doing their best, in subtle ways, to catch Sinjen's eye. "Oh! Who's the gentleman?" one called, causing more to come out and take an interest. Pretty women, but of a varied sort. Plenty stayed inside, so a fair few of them must have company already, Sinjen guessed. "He's beautiful. Did you bring him to us first?"

"Hell, no, he drinks like a fish, or he'd have been mine," Jack laughed. "Bring Sis."

A young woman dipped into the main building, returning with another, in puffed sleeves. A beauty, if older, her clothing gorgeous, fashionable, even in line with his own kind. Her dress was one of the latest women's suit designs, a look he found particularly endearing, the fabric elaborate and expensive, with a line of pretty dark buttons down her chest. She had a slender waist, and a neat hat, with a complimentary large silk bow.

"Incredible," he breathed, as Jack chuckled.

"What have you brought me tonight, Jack?" she said. Her voice was husky, but her expression proper. Her lips were thin, and only subtly painted.

"Ah. Someone who's more fun than he looks. You treat him special for me."

She laughed, "How much have you had to drink tonight? Are you staying with him?"

"I think so, I need a couch to doze on."

The woman shook her head at her brother, and gracefully approached Sinjen. He resisted the urge to touch her face when she was close enough. This Madam looked fierce yet proper, exactly his type. He smiled.

"What's your pleasure tonight, sir?" she asked, taking in his own neat suit.

"What do you recommend?"

She gave him a tight-lipped smile, little more than a wryly upturned corner, though her eyes had a warmth to them. "Follow me."

He followed her upstairs, dragging Jack by the arm. The drink was starting to catch up with the man. The Madam knocked on one of the doors. A sweet beauty opened it. She was hardly dressed, except for a lacy shift and violently green silk scarf, embroidered with cranes and lotus flowers. Her light brown hair, barely arranged, cascaded down her left shoulder.

"Penny. Make this one happy." She sighed, and turned to leave. Sinjen caught Carol's hand and pressed a gold sovereign into it. She looked at it and went to hand it to Penny, keeping it between her two hands.

Sinjen shook his head. "That's just for you. I like your hat."

She lowered her eyes and smiled demurely. "Make him very happy, Penny," she said, and returned to the main building.

Penny giggled and took him by the hand, the other still clutching her scarf for modesty. Jack ducked inside and threw himself onto her couch, as he'd indicated he would. Sinjen smiled and let the girl take him to her room. The whole place smelled of vanilla, coffee and clean linens. She must be popular – the other apartments couldn't all be this big, most would only be rooms. She turned and started to unbutton his frock coat, so he undressed himself.

"What am I doing?" he asked.

"Let me take a look at you first, and then, whatever you like," she said, sitting back on her bed, and watching him. "You're perfect, not a mark on you. How is that possible?"

He sighed. "I can't stay long, but I would."

"I believe you. Come back again, and I'll introduce you to my friends."

He kissed her, even if she was a little too young for his taste. Some fashions never changed, however tragically. He was a tragedy too: without other creatures of the night he'd have nothing, he borrowed their lives in more ways than one.

She stayed in her room afterwards. He went to Jack and mussed the man's hair before he left.

"Good?" Jack asked, waking from a light rest.

"Very good," Sinjen said and kissed him. The man kissed him back and put his arm on his shoulder, drawing him close. "What do you do for a living?"

"I look after Carol and the girls, with my friends. Rob a few too, on nights like this when everyone is out, or draw in punters."

"You're going to end up on the wrong end of a noose, I think. Do you want to come and work for me?"

"As what?"

"My valet. My last man left me." This wasn't true. Eliza had killed him out of boredom.

"Come back tomorrow, I'll let you know," Jack said, sliding his hand down his back. Sinjen stroked the front of Jack's trousers and heard him gasp. He too sighed, desire building, as he felt the blood pulse through Jack's member. He raised his hand, compelling the man to stillness, and sank his fangs into his throat, not taking too much, as Jack was already drunk. He licked the wound to stop the bleeding, and released his spell, letting Jack kiss him again before he pulled away.

"Sure. See you tomorrow. Keep out of trouble," he said, and went out.

A tired-looking woman passed him, carrying a few sheets. She was young, with a nice figure. Pretty, with dark hair, even if her expression was dour. 'What kind of woman ends up cleaning up after prostitutes?' he wondered, as he had before when visiting such an establishment. She was attractive enough to work as one, he supposed, and it would have to pay better, but perhaps this was the more moral option. Carol, at least, ran a tight ship. Her girls were clean and well cared for.

Old Memories

Chapter 2

He saw Carol on the way out and waved at her, placing her under a trance. "I need girls for tomorrow, but they won't come back. Where do I get them?"

"You'll have none of my girls," she replied, without seeing him. Sinjen decided he liked her even more than before. "Try the next street, the Madam there is ruthless."

He released her from his hold and thanked her for a pleasant night.

The next Madam was over-preened and false, but her girls were even prettier and more finely dressed than the last bevy. He arranged for a few party guests, and hypnotically suggested to her that they should be the least healthy ones. He could tell already that some had consumption. She agreed without reluctance and he departed, making sure to splash a generous amount at the bar. He'd need them to turn up. A handful of diseased whores wouldn't amuse his mistress enough, though she did favour women. He'd need a little more variety. A pair of nuns, perhaps, maybe a few fishermen or a surly bartender. He'd find something, but he'd only have a few hours.

He wandered around town with no particular destination in mind, until he spotted a pair of older men, who'd do well enough. "Musicians?" he asked.

"What gave you that idea?" one retorted, waving his guitar in Sinjen's general direction.

"Want to come to a party tomorrow?" he asked. "As guests, but play if you want to, and help yourselves to whatever you'd enjoy."

"Eh?" the other asked. "That doesn't sound right. What's the catch?"

"I'm employed by a crazy old rich woman, who likes to meet the peasantry from time to time." He sighed. "Doesn't matter that much who, but my job includes inviting people over."

"Right," the second one said, looking between Sinjen and his colleague. Sinjen had some doubts he would turn up. The first didn't seem to mind, but the intuition of the second had been set off.

"Come if you want, or don't," he said, told them the address, and pressed some currency into their hands. "For transport."

Fingers crossed, the first wouldn't come without the second and neither would show.

He did the same again to an old woman selling flowers. If Eliza had been human, his approach alone would have been enough to get her killed, but this wouldn't do it. Anyone with questions would be dismissed without trouble, or perhaps disappear themselves.

She'd never been cunning, just cruel, and always powerful. What star had she been born under? Marlais too had been hit with absurd good fortune, and delighted in suffering. He supposed they'd become despotic from this – ennui and excessive wealth. Poverty and weakness might have been a blessing to them, but they'd never really had either. At worst, a little justice served at the end of their lives. A dangerous pair together. God help him if they ever married, but they each hated the other sex with unfathomable bitterness. A shame in a sense, though – one or both would kill the other, he suspected, and he'd get to watch their friendship turn to venom.

He paused and took a deep breath. He could stand to eat again, but he couldn't be bothered. He'd have a thrall when he returned to the manor.

The clouds burst above him just as he'd been contemplating hailing a vehicle. Instead he ducked into a tea house. Nothing fancy, he'd thought, but it was nicer than he'd expected. Open at all hours to serve the rest houses nearby, the kinds of places where you could rent a bed some other shift worker had just vacated, or maybe a chair if you wanted to sleep sitting up and not touch the mattresses. There wasn't so much industry here, but enough, and the docks were busy at all hours one way or another.

The patrons were as he expected, exhausted labourers and night-shift workers. Others too, who, like him, had been out for the new year, now starting to flag in the small hours. He ordered a cup of tea, looking around as he waited in line. It was pouring outside and he didn't want to leave. Fortunately, at this time of year, he had a few more hours before dawn.

The tea house still had its Christmas decorations up, probably to be taken down at Twelfth Night. There was a live Christmas tree, prettily decorated with dried apple-slices on ribbons and colourful paper flowers. The whole room smelled of pine, mixed with tea and sweet spices.

Christmas trees hadn't been a tradition when he was young, but his sisters would have loved them. He could imagine the two young women laughing as they decorated one like it, but both had died of old age some years before. Perhaps they would have had one with their families when they'd started to become popular, and watched their grandchildren decorate them instead. He shook his head. How could something that had never been a part of his life have made him nostalgic?

He was told to take a seat, but the tea house was so busy. He looked around, peering over the heads of the other people and past the bright paper lanterns that decorated the place. Then he saw her, at the table by the window, her puffed sleeve partially submerged into the Christmas tree. It wasn't the tree, then, that had made him recollect his sisters, but her. Dark haired and quite plain, reading a book with a serious expression, half a cup of tea in front of her. She so closely resembled his cousin that they might have been related, her sleeves almost echoing the fashion of his own day. Yet she wore a dark boater hat instead of a bonnet and, to his amusement, a low rectangular pince-nez hanging from a black string.

"There are no empty tables, Miss. Might I join you?" he asked.

"You may, but I'm afraid I'll be poor company. I only want to read."

"That's perfect, so do I," he said, as she looked up at him. A flush rose to her cheeks when she saw how good-looking he was, but she returned to her book.

His tea was brought over and he offered to share the pot. She blushed again, but accepted.

"What are you reading?" he asked.

"*Dracula*, but if you want to talk, then wait until this chapter is finished."

He took his own book out and read for a bit too, or at least looked at the pages. He was really listening to the rain pelt against the window, and remembering other times.

"What are you reading?"

"*The Adventures of Sherlock Holmes*," he said, with a small smile.

"He's a strange character." She sighed.

"Is that one very scary? I know it's been popular with my friends, but I'm just a bit afraid of vampires."

She laughed, "Well, they aren't real, but no, it's not too bad. A little outrageous, perhaps."

"What do you mean?" he asked, taking in her appearance a little more closely. She was wearing some lace gloves, not suited to her style and not very warm. They were also torn, just on the inside of the thumb. She didn't have a single piece of jewellery on, and the string on her glasses was a little frayed.

"Well, the female vampires are a bit..."

"Seductive?" he asked.

"Well, I suppose you'll see when you read it."

"Would you like some cake?"

She looked up at him, raising her eyebrows.

"I could eat, but I'd feel bad if I ate on my own."

She smiled and folded her book away. "Alright."

When he'd ordered, he returned his attention to her. "I apologise, I never asked your name."

"I'm Miriam Green."

"I'm called Sinjen Carlyle." Then, "What's funny about Sherlock Homes?" he asked, after a moment.

She poured them both more tea. He noticed she was careful to conceal the hole in her glove as she did. "Isn't he addicted to cocaine? I don't know if I'd like him if we met. Well, I suppose I wouldn't even be interesting to him. Isn't anything outside of his work 'mere appendage'? I don't understand that. How could he know which parts of life would be relevant to him or not? Wouldn't life experience be useful to a detective?"

Sinjen considered her, a little amused. "I suppose you might be right. Personally, I only concern myself with life's appendage."

She looked at him wide-eyed, and her hand fluttered over her heart. "That's rather crude."

Sinjen laughed. "I'm sorry, I couldn't help it. I believe he calls everything else 'mere appendix'. Though I think I like your term better."

Miriam turned bright pink. "Oh, um, excuse me. I'm sorry."

"So, what do you do for a living?" he asked. "You must be a teacher or librarian, something like that?"

"Why those?"

"You've got ink-stained fingers. And, maybe, the reading glasses."

"I'm a shop clerk, but luckily I don't have work tomorrow."

"And I bet you come here all the time?" he said. A woman living alone on a meagre salary, he suspected. She'd be unable to keep her house warm this time of year. It would be easier to come out, and save on coal.

"I come here to read. My room still has gaslights, and rather temperamental ones, not electric bulbs like this. They're wonderful. But what do you do? Some made-up job, I bet, from your hands, like... um, a restaurant critic? No, I know, I bet you're a detective, but just for fun."

He laughed. She seemed a little childish, or perhaps overly imaginative, but must be at least twenty-six. "You're actually a little bit right. I used to be a kind of detective, but now I do private security work for an eccentric madwoman."

"She's eccentric *and* mad?" she asked.

"Yes, I'd have stuck with eccentric, but she's certainly got a few screws loose. It's a bit hard to forget."

"And you keep her safe?"

"That's right."

"You're related?" she asked.

"Not exactly. I suppose she's an in-law."

"You don't sound sure."

"Ah, she's the sister of my aunt. The rest of the family passed, but I'm not actually related to either of them. They live together, so I suppose I'm a sort of ward."

"Are they elderly?" Miriam asked.

"No, my aunt is much younger than me, but her sister is older."

"What a curious situation. Then, I suppose, you really do just float around doing as you please? If she doesn't need you."

"That's true, but she's very demanding. A big part of my job is keeping her entertained. You could meet her, if you like. She's throwing a big party tomorrow night. You could come as my guest?"

"I'd have nothing to wear," she said, dismissing the idea. Sinjen smiled, more relieved than he'd expected to be.

"I'm going to be busy tomorrow, but if I came here the night after, would I see you again?" The rain had slowed enough that he didn't mind leaving.

"Most likely, but not this late – around eight," she said, and returned to her book.

"Do you like vampires?" he asked,

"What's to like? They sound awful."

"You wouldn't want to meet some immortal true love, and spend an eternity together?"

She looked up at him and raised an eyebrow. "And kill people?"

"I suppose so," he said, resting his face on his hand. "But you would be a monster by then, so I imagine you wouldn't mind?"

"Then, I'd have lost my soul," she said, coldly.

"It's probably quite difficult to stay married for an eternity, too."

"I think marriage is difficult anyway."

"Not one of the world's great romantics then?" he said, smiling mischievously.

"Thank you for the Victoria sponge."

"You're very welcome. Goodnight, Miss Green."

He left, and started to look around for a carriage.

"Beep, beep," a statuesque man called, leaning against an automotive.

It was a little strange to see one of these novelties that had so recently become a fashion amongst the wealthy. This one had deep red seats, and looked something like an open-topped carriage which he'd neglected to attach horses to.

"Are you supposed to just *say* beep?" Sinjen sighed.

"I'm not going to honk the horn, am I? It's four in the morning. Anyway, hop in. I'm your lift home."

"Hmm." Sinjen sighed again, but walked over. Harry Balcom was easy enough company. He looked happy, as usual,and was wearing a flashy ditto suit, buttoned just at the top, which was rather a trend. "And *when* were you sent to find me?"

"Oh, at about the moment you left the party," he said sweetly, helping him climb in.

"So, you've followed me all night?"

"No, the first half of the night. I got a bit distracted at the whorehouse, and paid someone else to do it after that. Who's the girl?"

"All the tables were full, I don't know her," he said imploringly, as they drove out of town. "Please don't tell Eliza about her. I've really never seen her before."

"Oh, shut up. I didn't see a thing. Who was that fellow you were with?"

"I don't know, some thief, but don't get him killed either. I'm trying to hire a new valet."

"And you want a dashing young thief?" Harry laughed.

"Why the hell not?"

Harry didn't say anything, he was watching the road. He drove about as dangerously as expected – an immortal driving a metal vehicle was such a bad idea. Sinjen gripped the car seats as they swerved to avoid some rabbits.

"Are they supposed to go this fast? I thought they only went about twelve miles an hour."

Harry chuckled. "Hell, no. It's not supposed to do this, but it turns out they do, if you levitate the carriage. I want to ask you for some advice when you have time. You know I'm staying with you for a while? Well, with Eliza. So come out with me, next time. Of course, I'll be temporarily blind again, just like tonight."

"Thank you," he said coldly.

Harry patted his knee.

"Can you keep your bloody hands on the stick please!"

"Reckon I can drive with my feet?" He laughed, and watched the horror flit across Sinjen's face.

The Little Princess

Chapter 3

Harry let Sinjen out of the car when they got back to Eliza's mansion, a Georgian country house with high ceilings and a stunning cottage garden. He'd been allowed free rein over the outdoors, and even chosen the north of the country. Eliza cared little for planting. As long as she had space to entertain, she'd said he could do as he pleased. Sinjen had asked the gardeners to do whatever they wanted. If the house had been safe for the public, he'd have loved to open it up so that people could visit and see what they'd created. Even more, he'd love to see it during the day, but at least it was a favourite of green carpet and brimstone moths. He took a few deep breaths and prepared to go inside. His hair was a mess after the car ride, so he neatened it with a look of extreme displeasure.

"You okay, man?" Harry asked, clapping him on the back.

Sinjen shot him a furious look. Harry only laughed and dragged him inside.

Eliza was waiting for him in the main reception room. The servants were tidying up. Most likely, there was a room full of unconscious vampires upstairs already.

"And *how* was your night?" she said, her voice as chilling as usual.

"It was eventful enough, my darling one," Sinjen told her, "I ran into a gang of thieves and drank them under the table. And yours, my love?"

She frowned and looked towards Harry. "Is this the truth?"

"Yes, dearest Princess. He went to a couple of whorehouses and watched the sea, but nothing of particular note."

"I was looking for some guests as well, my darling, for tomorrow."

Eliza nodded to dismiss Harry, then beckoned Sinjen to come closer. He knelt before her and she rested her foot on his shoulder. "I need you to send for my dressmaker. I'm running out of party clothes, and I want some lace or something on my collar, something less tame. These modern styles are so *dull*, especially for events, but at least the sleeves are finally worth a damn again."

"My darling, order something with ruffs, something elaborate, whatever you desire. I have an idea for some parties that would suit our own fashions. That would be fun, wouldn't it?"

She looked down her nose at him, almost approvingly, and shoved the heel of her boot into his shoulder; he winced, but pressed into it.

"Very well. Go to bed," she instructed.

He stood, bowed low and left.

"Sinjen!" a sweet voice called from a bedroom, as he walked through the upstairs corridor.

"Little Princess?" he answered, from outside the door. He hadn't thought he'd made any noise, but she'd have stayed up all night, probably pinching cakes from the kitchens.

"Come in!"

Margaret was inside with her current attendant, this being Sora Skinner, one of the Nightfall knights. A shapely redhead, prone to occasional extremes of good nature and fleeting intimacy.

Though Nightfall was not based in England, most of the English vampires who belonged to them lived in their own country. They were sent for by letter, or nowadays even by telephone, though those were still something of a novelty. They had one, but if he was being honest they kind of unnerved him. Margaret enjoyed them, though, as did the other vampire children.

Sinjen nodded at Sora, who ignored him, and asked Margaret about her night.

"It was a good night. Carlotta called to say she is coming over tomorrow for a visit, and I wrote in my diary, but don't you dare read it. It's over there on the table, the one with the pink cover."

"Oh, I see, so I *shouldn't* read it and learn all your secrets?"

She grinned, watching Sora roll her eyes but hurry to take the book before Sinjen got there.

She flicked through it carefully, then sighed and handed it to Sinjen. "Very amusing."

"This is like no diary I've ever seen," Sinjen admitted, leafing through the pages.

"It's the diary of all the bugs I've seen this month. I thought you'd like to see the cinnabar moth."

"That's a very chubby caterpillar, rather happy-looking eyes."

"Thank you. I hope he was happy when I was drawing him, because afterwards I put him on the bird table."

"You're almost as cruel as your dear sister," he chuckled.

24

"Well, we can't prove he didn't deserve it."

"Guilty until proven innocent," Sinjen agreed.

Sora cleared her throat. "Shut up, or I'm letting Eliza know."

"She might like to see my drawings," Margaret said with a cheeky grin. "Oh, Sinjen, we also had a letter from our missing friend."

"Oh, the annual, 'I'm not dead'?"

"That's it. Sora already approved it."

"There's nothing in it, but I don't like it," Sora said, a note of warning in her voice.

Sinjen went to read the unremarkable, uncrumpled, but slightly bloodstained letter. A smear of dirt on the edge suggested that he'd made an effort to clean the outside, but the interior of the message was pristine. Handwriting near neat enough to rival his own, if less frilly:

"Dearest Aunt,

I hope my letter finds you well. I killed a dozen ghouls last week, and if it turns out to be your sister again, I'll kill her too. Please remind Sinjen he's a prat.

Lots of love, your living nephew."

"About as verbose as usual," he said.

"But at least my sister is probably alive."

"Well, that's nice."

"The time, Sinjen!" Sora called and stood to leave, so that Margaret's day minder could take over, a young thrall who couldn't do more than watch her. There was no way to stop Margaret if she wanted to escape. It was more that there really wasn't anywhere she could go, and no future for her, if she did seriously leave. She'd be without her family and, as a child, have very few ways to support herself. She could probably do it, but not for very long.

"Stay here longer," Margaret suggested. "I can keep you safe in the daytime."

Sinjen frowned. "Come to my room for a bit, if you want to talk a little more."

"You know I can watch you sleeping whenever I like, don't you?"

"Please don't do that, and don't say things like that."

"I'll come with you," Margaret said, following him out.

When Sinjen was sitting on his bed, Margaret asked what was on her mind, even though her keeper stood outside Sinjen's door to listen. The wind was howling outside. Every now and then, a draft blew down the chimney, sending a chill throughout the room. Sinjen didn't need a fire and, as he had no thrall, nobody had bothered to light one. The night's weather had been so unsettled, at least after midnight.

Margaret dimly wondered if it was the smoke from the fireworks that caused the change in the weather, or else, it was only January. She thought the day might be nicer than the dawn, but for now, it was still dark enough that they had a few extra moments to speak.

"Are you happy, Sinjen?"

"How can I be happy, Margaret?" he asked, his voice already weakening as the sky brightened a little.

"You ought to meet someone. Someone who'll make you feel human again. You've been through so much, and you might actually be able to now."

"I'd just get her killed."

"They're only food anyway, Sinjen. What does it matter if you do?" she asked.

"It would just be more grief to me."

"Then keep her safe. You're good enough at protecting yourself. You have some friends now. If nothing else, you'll learn what you're capable of." She could tell his resistance was wearing away, and his eyelids were starting to grow heavy. He slid under his sheets, still fully dressed, in the sensible neutral shades he was so prone to. They did suit him well. He was too lovely to need much emphasis. He always reminded her a little of a nightingale. A perfect little creature of darkness. Harmless, yet a friend of death himself, according to the whispers. A longtime companion of suffering.

"I did talk to a sweet woman tonight," he said, his breath faltering.

"Reminded you of Carlotta?" she guessed.

"Reminded me of everything."

"She sounds nice," Margaret said, and kissed him gently on his forehead, just at the moment his breathing ceased.

As she left, she called her thrall. The young woman's eyes were slightly misted over. Margaret knew she'd secretly adored Sinjen for a fair while. Incidentally or not, Charlotte had only ever seen his sweet side, and few ever did. "Will you tell Eliza he contemplated an affair, Charlotte?" she asked.

"I didn't hear anything like that," she said, wiping her eyes, "I think if he fell in love, even a little, it would do wonders for him."

Margaret let out a little, childish laugh. "It'll never happen, but even contemplating love would be good for him. Take me to the sweetshop today. I want to see if they still have those little green sweets they make with arsenic."

Charlotte giggled, not much more than a girl herself. "Oh, alright, but only if you treat me to some chocolates."

"I shall, because you're so good to my sweet nephew."

"Nephew?"

"Just a little joke," Margaret giggled, "He's barely a lifetime old and I have my centuries, did you forget?"

"It's easy to forget, dear Princess."

Princess of the Night

Chapter 4

"You look beautiful, my darling. I don't understand why you don't like the style, actually. Isn't it closer to your own day, even than to mine? Mutton-chop sleeves and full skirts?" He watched Eliza pose and rehearse a few of her more common gestures in one of her newer dresses, checking the fit. She'd had this one for a little while, but never worn it.

"God, you're a fool. Can't you recognise an A-line? And the neckline, it's atrocious. The material is just *ghastly*. Machine-made, *really*? What *will* they think of next? They'll be letting the serfs wear any fabric they like."

"Um, actually, Mistress..." he attempted, his expression conflicted. She glared at him, and he instantly gave up. "My darling, you can have anything you desire. If you want the fabric printed or embroidered, it's easier now than ever, any colour, from any country. Even whole sheets of lace. It should just keep getting better, shouldn't it?"

Eliza wasn't pretty, not for a vampire. Nor was she very tall, but she was about as imperious and grandiose as it was possible for a person to be. It was always a mistake to forget how hard-hearted she was, or to misjudge one of her moods or impulses. He was one of the few people who could make her laugh, and she only did that sparingly unless there was pain involved.

"Ah," she said, jerking her hand to the side, and yawned. "Mark me. Things will change, and then they won't. It'll be a free-for-all for a few minutes. *Then,* one way or another, there will be a uniform for the drudges, and a whole separate system for us. They'll find another way to worship us, and we will find *other* ways to blend in. The foolish ones will flash their lucre, and we will conceal ourselves, only pausing to show off to one another. *What* was your party idea?"

"Vampires. We're in vogue now. Perhaps a masquerade?"

She smiled, "I like it. Bring me one of the girls. I want to make her dance."

Sinjen bowed and fetched one, though their next party would start soon. A hapless scullery maid was who his eye caught first. He watched, showing no sign of any sentiment, as Eliza, who had removed her outer clothing in his absence, forced her to disrobe and step into a cage. Eliza suspended it above herself and slashed at the girl's feet and legs with knives, until she, licking the soles of the girl's feet, had been amused enough.

Sinjen held a towel for her afterwards while she bathed. Thank the Lord that demonic woman was small, or else he'd have had to fetch two for her to have been covered in enough blood to satisfy her. The girl had survived, though weakened, and weeping from fear and pain. She was carried away, to recover.

He helped Eliza to dress, lacing and buttoning her into a black gown with dramatic gold sleeves, their puffs falling heavily and artistically yet maintaining the popular form. Sinjen sent for the girl who did her hair. Her fingers were still bandaged from her last mistake, but she styled Eliza's hair in a series of elaborate twists and curls. Having been adorned with enamelled flower pins, Eliza swept out into the gardens. When she was gone the girl began to cry, her repressed fear finally safe to express.

Sinjen reached towards her, but the young woman only backed away, and he was reminded that he was Eliza's monster. That young lady was at as much risk as the last when it came to Eliza's desires. He made a mental note to recruit another hairdresser before he changed for the party. That one wouldn't last very long.

He slipped into a more formal suit, of more expensive fabric, light in colour with a cream waistcoat. He prayed, as he did each time, that his guests would turn up, and that he'd stumbled across lowlifes worthy of death. He was aware that there was no chance he could possibly be blameless, not after all this time. He put on the marigold boutonnière that Margaret had made for him and went to join the others.

The party was in full swing when he arrived. Lady Margaret had retired to her room, never allowed to attend. The view of vampire children was that, if they would stay children, then it would mean they were treated that way. Better seen and not heard, though he'd never dare say that to Margaret's face.

The garden was beautiful. The electric lights made it stunning at night, brightening the tree branches and highlighting the few plants that bloomed at night. He'd long ago requested that the planting would include areas for lovers and trysts. As a consequence, the grounds were full of unusual winding paths. He loved the style so much. Good-sized patches of one particular flower, then another, interspersed with a few vegetables, fruit trees or shrubbery. The total effect was one of controlled chaos, but practical. He knew Lady Margaret had started a side business of selling their produce to a local grocer. Eliza, though brutally astute when it came to the finances of her household, did not extend her interest past the kitchen gardens. He had some doubts as to whether she'd know a carrot from a hogweed. She'd never notice a crop of missing potatoes from the edge of a flowerbed.

He exited through the kitchen entrance and took a leisurely stroll towards the heart of the party.

"No, don't touch me there!" called Sora with delight from behind an artistically braided screen of willow. He suppressed his laughter in time – that was the voice she used when her breasts were fondled, and the laugh. "Please, definitely don't put your hand right there!" She giggled, and he heard the laughter of her male companion as he called her something quite impolite.

He walked on, but paused to listen when he heard a familiar voice.

"But you don't understand. He'd never let anyone know! And you, you can't tell him. It's not safe. You don't know him like I do."

Then, Harry Balcom's laugh. "And what, pray, can he do about it?"

"You'll see, please. Don't even go near him, and never let him find out. If you value your life; even mine."

"But, my dear, we will be together. It's inevitable. I knew it the moment I saw y—" then he was silenced, cut off by Carlotta's kiss.

Sinjen shook his head. As if he didn't already know, but it made no difference to him. As long as Eliza never discovered the depths of his affection for Carlotta, she should be safe. As far as he knew, almost no one outside of Daylight had ever found out that they had been close when they were alive. He shut his eyes for a moment. The memory of her, smiling in the sun and pressing her lips against his. Knowing that she'd never even kissed another man and would willingly be his forever. It crept up on him from time to time, but she was gone. His sweet... even her real name.

He passed a few other conversations and dalliances of no particular note (except that some involved the girls he had sent for), until he came across Lord Marlais and Eliza, just concealed from him. He listened for a moment, poised to flee if there was any sign they might hear him.

"But he bores me now," Eliza sighed, "He works hard but he—"

"There has never been anyone so devoted to you." Marlais sighed, and Sinjen knew he must be holding her, as he so often did. "Test him, if you wish. Watch him. He loves you. You've made your will his entire focus and he fears you too much to ever question it. You'd be a fool to lose him without reason."

"Nonsense. He'll betray me."

Marlais laughed. "Test him, then, don't wonder. He's as bad as us – in a few centuries he'll be a legend too. The others already fear him, but we don't need to."

"They fear *me*, Gilles. He is as false as the day is long, and just as deadly."

Marlais sighed. "Don't guess. I'll help you think of something."

Sinjen spirited to the front door of the house. That was dangerous. Eliza was bored and Marlais was amusing himself. He could do nothing without risk.

He pressed his back against the wall and thought for a while, fishing a cigarette out of the case which Margaret had given him for his fiftieth.

33

Though, lost as he was, he hadn't realised it was his birthday gift. It had waited until he got out of Nightfall's dungeon again.

He'd smoked the first one before he remembered a simple truth. *You're property, and until she is dead conduct yourself as such. Eliza dies before Marlais.*

He walked back to the party, his expression ice-cold.

At least when he was in a bad mood it was fun to watch the other vampires tiptoe. Nobody bothered him, they just let him smoke in peace. They were trying not to catch his eye, in case he was looking for some treason, or cruel distraction Eliza would enjoy. He did know that someone had been stealing, but Marlais had brought his latest wife to the party, so for now Eliza should be occupied. Every so often, he'd let his eye rest on someone or other for a little while and, if he felt like it, grin as he took a drag.

He sighed. Someone had missed the brief. Harry kept winking at him and waving him over. Carlotta had gone to speak with some other women, but she was his focus of attention. He kept trying to catch her eye. His amused smile, as he tried to find ways to do it, was a little sweet. Carlotta couldn't be oblivious to this, but he knew her well enough to know she'd make him work for her attention.

One of the annoyances of being a vampire was their hierarchy. Even though Sinjen, strictly speaking, only answered to Eliza, or those who could still command her, it was still uncomfortable to try to ignore the whims of a more powerful vampire. Even if they were not from the same clan.

As it was now, he was still young. Harry had two hundred years and a rank over him. Having put it off for as long as he could tolerate, he shot the man an irritated glare and finally went over to him.

"What?"

"What, Sir Balcom. Please," Harry corrected, with a grin. "It would be your great pleasure to read this poem to the fair Carlotta, on my behalf."

"Right." He sighed, noting, if nothing else, that Eliza was watching him with amusement. He hadn't heard anything positive about Harry's creative efforts.

He scanned the poem briefly. The *absolute* cheek of the man, it looked like he'd even made a bit of an effort with it too.

He walked over to Carlotta and exhaled loudly, before he began:

"*Princess of the Night, by Sir Henry Balcom.*"

He watched Carlotta grin, but shoot an unimpressed glance at Harry, who returned an enthusiastic wave. It was known that Sinjen and Carlotta had a complex relationship, generally considered to be a strong rivalry, one which Sinjen was losing. So, before he'd even started, he'd drawn a crowd.

"*Princess of—*"

"A bit more showmanship, Sinjen," Harry requested.

Sinjen obliged, with a more dramatic and emotional read:

"*Princess of the night, sweetest of all flowers,*
my perfect blood-red rose, seen then never forgotten
from the first moment until the last.
Fair one, echo of a gentle past, you keep my soul in torment.
My heart wishes to foment a union unending,
as undying as our hearts.
My dear, humour me, even in jest,
although I am truly grotesque. In the trouser department, unblessed,
and so often dispossessed, that they say I have less than a gelding."

"Hold on, I didn't end it like that. Sinjen, how could you? I spent *minutes* on that, I even cried a little."

Carlotta was laughing silently into her hands.

"Oh my. I guess I accidentally replaced that line with one that rhymed." He handed the original poem to Carlotta, who read the real ending, then gave Harry a disapproving look.

"Well, of course he wouldn't read that out, but it was rather pretty."

Sinjen rolled his eyes, and went back to smoking.

The real poem had been:

"Princess of the night, sweetest of all flowers,

my perfect blood-red rose, seen then never forgotten

from the first moment until the last.

Fair one, echo of a gentle past, you keep my soul in torment.

My heart wishes to foment a union unending,

as undying as our hearts.

Forget your loss unexpressed,

that lamented unworthy unblessed, for our immortal wedding.

I'll take your breath away, and always give you more."

The idea of asking the cause of her suffering to read the poem... and a proposal no less. The absolute nerve. He was unworthy, but Harry had only recently arrived in England. Though Harry and Carlotta were in the same clan, Harry had spent most of the last century in Vietnam. So, how long had he known her? He'd have to make enquiries.

Eliza had laughed at the diversion, but as she and Marlais were starting to make his latest wife fearful, he'd be occupied for the rest of the night. He'd have to start by making sure the band was playing loudly enough to drown out her screams.

The Man in the Wolf Fur Collar

Chapter 5

S injen wanted very much to leave. Eliza was with her dressmaker, and while he'd already asked to go out tonight, if he reminded her while she was absorbed, she'd take offence. Consequently, he was stuck holding fabric swatches against one of the maids who had similar colouring: black hair and very fair skin.

Keeping Eliza supplied with female domestic servants would be a significant burden on its own, if it didn't amuse her to do it herself. He suspected that cruelty alone wasn't what she fixated on, but the girls. She liked to find a fresh clutch of young women, entice them to work for her, and slowly torment them until none remained. For all that she disliked men, there was something about having power over pretty girls that could absorb her focus like nothing else. She could take months to get rid of them all, but she liked a constant supply or she became very unpleasant, very quickly.

The other girl in the room, sitting at Eliza's side, might actually have a chance of surviving. A curiously dark-skinned girl for England, possibly the daughter of someone who'd had dealings in Jamaica, but it was hard to guess her exact heritage. She was pretty, which helped, with rosy lips and wide blue eyes. Though innocent looking, she was not. She'd been shrewd enough to identify the best way to survive his Lady –adopting slavish devotion, mixed with extreme cruelty to anyone else in the group, before Eliza had even noticed that it was a deliberate tactic.

She was currently holding a book full of designs for her, and would occasionally make a complementary suggestion. He did not like this; it was a dangerous form of competition.

If she'd turned up, even five years ago, he'd have arranged her death by now. Today, if he could have her fill the void for him, without incident, then Eliza might actually get used to him not being around.

The girl, Laura, looked up at him for a moment. Her expression was almost as unreadable as his own, and he was afraid that she was considering similar things. His expression became more guarded.

There was a knock on the door and Harry breezed in. "Evening, Elder Eliza. Can I borrow Sinjen?"

"*Why?*" she asked, barely looking up from her sample fabrics.

"We both need new servants. Two birds and all that."

"Oh. Very well," she said.

Sinjen bowed and left. He saw Laura smile slightly as he did.

"Hey, did you forget we were going out?" Harry asked as they drove away.

Sinjen, who had been lost in thought, his expression troubled, looked up and brightened significantly. "No. I just couldn't get away without making her angry, I could tell."

"Oh. I thought I'd upset you. You looked like you were planning to kill me when I knocked. You aren't annoyed about the poem?"

"Why would I be? You wanted to ask me about getting her attention or something, didn't you?" Sinjen asked. He fished a cigarette out of his case, growing more cheerful.

"I never told you that."

"You did. Just not with words. Besides, the number of Moonlight fellows who come to me for relationship advice, especially if it's about Carlotta—"

"Really, which ones?" Harry said, turning to him with a very concerned expression. Sinjen laughed. "And, you gave them advice, or...? Just, I can get her into bed without any trouble, but I don't think she really wants me."

"No offence, Sir Henry, but I can't imagine why she would. You have a reputation..."

"Well, look, just because people think I'm a spendthrift, a gambler, womaniser and general wastrel, that doesn't mean I'd be a bad prospect."

Sinjen rubbed his eyebrow with one hand and shook his head.

"Well, exactly," Harry continued, "She does that too, when I say so. So that's why I need the help. Or what? You would rather screen me first?"

"Maybe I should," Sinjen sighed.

"Fine. We have a bit of time before you are to meet your bland woman, so let's try that house of ill-repute first. We need to take some measurements, and I'm sure someone there has a ruler. Not that I don't already know I'll win – who *hasn't* seen you naked?"

Sinjen rolled his eyes. "How did you know I wanted to see her?"

"Aww, Carlyle, I can read people too. You looked like a lovesick schoolgirl, leaning on the table with that goofy grin. I didn't know your face did that."

Sinjen became guarded and watchful. "Yeah, that's the face I'm used to, and the mean one."

When they arrived at their intended establishment, they were ushered directly into their best private room. "How much did you spend here?" Sinjen asked.

"I don't know, I wasn't counting." Harry shrugged.

The Madam came in with a couple of girls, but she was disturbed. Her hands trembled as she waved the girls in, and she kept glancing back through the open door.

Sinjen asked her what was wrong. "We had some trouble earlier tonight. Our... Jack and his friends got hurt, we had to send for a doctor."

Sinjen took her hands. He could tell she wouldn't have told him anything, except that it had happened recently and she was still processing it.

He sent the girls out for a few moments, while Harry lounged on one of the couches and helped himself to a drink.

"So, tell me what happened?" Sinjen asked. "Are they okay?"

Harry raised an eyebrow.

"Well, yes, but all were hurt, and Archie might— The doctor thinks it might be fine, but it'll take a while to be sure. He's cleaned the injury up. A broken bottle –it was only one man, but he was very impassioned," she said, struggling not to cry.

She took a handkerchief out of her pocket before Sinjen had even reached for his. He noted, again, how neat and pretty the way she moved was.

"Tell me what happened, from the beginning. When did the trouble start?"

"He came into the main building. That part was fine, but he didn't drink. He started looking around for one of the girls, he had no interest in anything else. So, our men tried to stop him, but he got more and more riled up. He kept calling for someone named Viola. We don't have a girl by that name. When we tried to tell him so, he started to panic, swearing blind that she was here. Insisted he had to see her, it was life or death. Then this fight happened, and he ran.

"We didn't call the police, of course, but a number of our patrons, well, they are police, so... When they threw their weight around, this man fled. Only afterwards did I realise who he was looking for. Not one of the girls, but our cleaning woman. Nobody thought of her straight away. She wasn't in just then; she'd taken a basket of sheets to be laundered."

"Is she back now?" he asked.

"I can check, sir, but why do you ask?"

"I do some private security work. I could look into it."

Carol shot him an uncertain glance. "Is that true? Do you have a licence?"

"Of course," he said, and hypnotised her into believing that she'd seen it. "I should speak to your brother too, if it's alright."

Carol nodded, and left the room.

"Do you actually care?" Harry asked. "This isn't our problem."

"It doesn't have to be *your* problem at all," Sinjen pointed out, "but why wouldn't I care?"

"You're bored?"

"My new friend was glassed. I'm allowed to eat the guy who did it, if I want to. It can't be that hard to find him."

Harry sat up and looked at him over. "You actually do care, don't you? Who the hell worries about some random Madam? This kind of thing probably happens every other night."

"I doubt it's over the cleaning lady."

"She'll be a whore on the side," Harry said, leaning back on the couch.

"He took out three men at once over her, and they're pretty worldly fellows."

"Oh, I'll bet," Harry said, pouring himself a little more wine. "You like the Madam too, don't you? Which do you prefer, her or her brother? She's not so good-looking either. Is it plain girls in general that you like? Ah, do they work harder?"

"Shut up, Harry."

"You should be nicer to me if you want to play detective. I can help you get out of the house when you like."

"You're just swell, Harry."

"I am. Thank you, and...?"

"Bigger than me?" he guessed.

Harry grinned.

Madam Carol returned with the woman he'd noticed before, pretty and meek. She didn't want to be in the room and looked especially wary of Harry, who stood the moment he saw her and bowed. Carol stayed by her side.

"I won't waste your time, Mrs...?" he began.

"Miss Webb." she said timidly, "I..."

"There's no need to worry, Miss Webb. I'm not a policeman. I only want to make sure everything is alright. Could this man have been pursuing you at one time?"

She flushed, and looked away. "I don't know how he could have found me. I think, there's only one person who... who it might have been, but I didn't see him."

Carol spoke up, "Tall, well-built, light blond hair and ice-blue eyes."

Viola winced. "A foreigner? Probably wore a thick fur collar, and had scars across his face and hands? Like, like a wolf had done it... almost?"

"That would be him. Why would you know such a person, Viola?"

She didn't look like she wanted to say.

"Excuse me, good lady," Harry suggested, "you might be embarrassed, but I doubt any one of us can claim a moral high ground. I don't think your employer would think less of you."

Viola glanced at Carol, who nodded. "This sort of thing happens too often here, but it's not your fault how someone else carries on."

Viola took a deep breath. "When I was a young woman, I worked in a... a guest house of sorts. It was our own. Some people would stay for years at a time, others only a night. This was about ten years ago; I was fifteen then. A strange family came through, all with scars and very secretive. They rented a large section of the house and stayed for a long time.

"They were injured often, but always dealt with it themselves. They even paid us more not to talk about them and not to ask questions. The mother only had one arm, but their son, then, was rather beautiful. He

43

was hurt one day, brought home, close to death, and I remember being so terrified for him. I do know that he should have had large slashes across his face and neck." She drew her fingers across where they would be on her own face, to illustrate their location. Carol nodded to confirm this. "They were very wealthy, by the way, and I found them so fascinating and exotic.

"By the time a year had passed, my mother threw me out, because I... myself and the young man... We had wanted to marry, but his father wouldn't hear of it. I had nowhere to go, and allowed the boy's father to pay me off. I didn't have another option. I don't believe he ever even found out. I told Mother first, but that was my mistake.

"I have a little still of what his father gave me, to this day. Put away for my son's schooling, and I work to keep us afloat. Miss Carol has always been good about it. Night work pays quite well, and I can still see my son during the day. I... I could have said I was a widow and changed my name, or married, but I wrote an old friend from those days. He told me that the young man, now grown, of course, had been looking for me. According to this friend, he'd never given up on our being reunited.

"This was years ago. Until tonight, I thought I was a fool for wanting to see him again. I can't imagine how he could have felt, if he found out I worked here... Or what he might have thought. I hope he's alright. I'm sorry for what he did, but if I had to guess, if he was afraid, then he had a reason. That's not an excuse. I mean, he was never prone to fear."

"Thank you, Miss," Sinjen said and let her go.

Carol apologised, and returned to her brother.

"What a charming young lady, that Viola. She has something about her, doesn't she?" Harry said, with a gentle sort of admiration. "Did you notice her before?"

"Yes, but what did that boy sound like to you?"

Harry grinned. "You really have a nose for this. I'd have missed the story by a mile, but you'll only miss your lady, if you don't leave soon."

"Damn it. I should check on Jack, too."

"I'll check in on him for you. That way I can tell Eliza that we looked at some potential thralls today. He'll be safe, don't worry."

"Tell him I'll come and see him later, but why are you acting like my friend?" Sinjen asked, turning back to him.

"I've known you for ages. Did you never notice me? I even came to visit you in the Moonlight dungeons. Brought you a book of erotic woodcuts. You didn't talk to me, though."

Sinjen blinked at him. "When my vision came back, those were quite entertaining."

"Oh, was that why? You did look a sight. I wanted to have a look at you while I was in town. You caught my interest again when I heard about you and Isolde. I've kept an eye on you."

Sinjen frowned, but only straightened his tie and left.

Miriam was in the cafe, but so absorbed by her book that she didn't see him. He watched her absently dip a biscuit into her tea, then hold it uneaten for long enough that it fell onto the table. She sighed and tidied it up.

"Is that a good bit?" he asked.

"It's quite thrilling," she admitted, her expression a little sheepish.

"Have you already eaten? I haven't."

"No, not yet. I was going to, but I lost track of time."

"I think I know a nice place," Sinjen said, gesturing towards the door. She turned to him, wary, almost fearful. For just a second, Sinjen was cut to the quick, afraid she had somehow sensed who he was. He didn't have to worry for long. Miriam dipped her head and gave him a timid smile, making everything feel right again.

The Landlady

Chapter 6

Sinjen took Miriam out for a steak pie and mulled wine. They didn't eat it at the vendor, but on the path towards St. Mary's. They stopped at a bench with a nice view of the road leading down to the town. It had been a slight walk, but both felt it had been worth it. They'd skipped a couple of the benches, because one had a coffin on it. The men who'd been carrying it up the hill to the cemetery had given up for the evening and left the poor soul to enjoy the view. That couldn't be usual at this time of evening, but no one would bother whoever it was anyway. At least, Sinjen hoped that the market for organs wouldn't be a problem out here.

He began to relax, taking in the sea breeze at her side. The sounds of amusement and the early night bustle drifted up to them from the town. Every so often, the echoing cry of a seagull or two cut over everything else. Whitby really was charming, and a very distinctive shape, between the hills and the curve of the coastline. Even though the North Sea was regarded with suspicion, its large beach and seaside attractions were a draw by themselves.

This wasn't the kind of seaside destination people visited for their health, though he supposed they might. This was the newer style of resort town, where people came to play, tour and explore the country. Much like Blackpool, it was courting people's free time. It was a pleasure to watch, and so different from vampiric society that he almost felt protective of the lighthearted atmosphere.

"This must be a nice place to live," he said, watching the visitors still strolling around the promenade. Miriam smiled, and admitted that it was.

When they had eaten and Miriam had finished the last of her drink, her eyelids drooping very slightly, he leant over and kissed her. He drew back, and the two stared at each other, equally wide-eyed.

"Oh, my God. I'm so sorry, please forgive me," Sinjen said, speaking first.

Miriam blushed, and covered her face with both hands.

"Are you okay?"

She laughed. "It's alright. It was only a kiss, but why did you do it?"

He smiled and gazed at the sea before he was ready to answer. "I couldn't help it. You were so content."

She laughed again. "You sound so ashamed. It's okay. I, um, I never thought you'd... kiss me."

"Why?"

"You're beautiful. I'm only..."

"Clever? Funny? Excuse me, but, do you live alone? Where are your parents?"

"They died. I'm on my own now, but it's alright. I miss them, of course, but it's been this way for a few years now. I'm used to getting by. I was lucky to find decent work. I suppose I might marry someday, and it'll be different."

"I see."

"Um. You aren't married?" she asked.

"I wouldn't be kissing young ladies if I was," he laughed.

"You aren't that much older than me. Or younger?"

"I'm older than I look," he said and kissed her again, but only on the cheek.

"You should probably stop that. Will you walk me home?"

He agreed, and they wandered back into town. Her room was a fair way from the tea house where she went to read; it was actually closer to where Harry still was. To his surprise, she invited him to see her apartment, and as a vampire he accepted. It just wasn't the kind of thing he'd turn down.

There was an old lady knitting in the hallway, sucking a sherbet lemon. "No gentleman callers!" she barked at Miriam as they passed.

"It's alright, Nettie. I don't think he is a gentleman."

"That's alright then," Nettie agreed, and offered Sinjen one of her sweets. He accepted.

"Who is she?" he asked, when they were out of earshot.

"My landlady. She's only teasing me, because she's always got a man over and I never bring anyone home. Careful of her, though, she'll eat you alive."

Sinjen raised an eyebrow. "She sounds great. Why did you invite me here?"

She unlocked the door and they went in. Her room was astonishingly bare. Unpainted brick walls and an unlit fireplace, with not a lot of fuel next to it. In the corner was the table that she used to prepare food. There wasn't much on that either, just bread, jam and a jar of potted shrimp. There was also a washbasin, a narrow wardrobe and a thin, but very soft-looking bed. It seemed that the only thing she really spent money on were her books. She had a full bookshelf, and there were a few more stacks on the windowsill and against the wall, where they functioned as a makeshift side table. The room was very neat, big enough to look sparse, but not especially comfortable. He went to look at the books while she turned on the gas lamps. She hadn't lied, they were rather dim, even though she turned them up.

"Would you like a cup of tea?" she asked.

"No, thank you." He didn't especially want her to light the fire on his account. "It's quite a warm night for January, isn't it?"

She chuckled. "I, um, I don't know exactly why I invited you back here. Well, except that you seemed like you'd be interested to know how I live. Another man might have made me nervous, asking a question like that, but you did only seem curious. Do you want to borrow any books?"

"Actually, may I? You've got some romances I haven't read yet."

"I thought you'd want *Dracula*."

"I actually have read that. I just wanted to talk to you before."

"Do you have any plans for the rest of the night?" she asked, coming over to him and looking politely at the two books he'd chosen. They were two of the more fanciful romances. "You're quite sweet, aren't you? You haven't even tried to kiss me again."

"You said I shouldn't."

"I like that you listened." She took his hand and led him over to the bed, "This is the best place to sit, if you're wondering. I'm not after anything, if that's alright. I just want to talk."

"It's still a bit scandalous," he said, smiling very slightly.

"I know, but one of the advantages of having no living family is that there's nobody to care. It's the same for you, right? Nobody minds what you get up to?"

"I'm afraid my aunt Eliza cares a great deal. She's also my employer. I don't have much free time. So, believe it or not, this is a bit of an adventure for me."

"She doesn't like you to meet women?" she asked, wide-eyed.

"No. I can't marry either, maybe I should tell you so..."

She covered her mouth with her hand and gasped. "She treats you like her lover?"

He winced. "I am her lover. I can't really do much about that. I can't leave – don't ask about why. Suffice it to say, I wouldn't be left in peace. I'd like to see you more, but I don't know if I'd be able to do that very often."

"I see." She sighed.

"Hey, do you want to be my mistress? It should be pretty easy, considering you'll probably never see me. You don't have to sleep with me, either, I'd just enjoy having one."

She laughed. "That's ridiculous, I could never!"

"No, I didn't think you would," he said, amused.

"Did you only ask me because I'm not so well-off?" she asked, looking at the floor.

"Well, for several reasons. I'd quite like to kiss you a few more times and keep a secret from my aunt. Finding excuses to spend money is kind of tiring."

"What were you doing before you came to meet me?"

"I was commissioned to solve a mystery," he said with a wry smile.

"Can I help?"

"Yes, if you like, but I insist on paying for your time and expenses."

"That sounds fun." She laughed.

"Oh good. In that case, light the fire and I'll tell you all about it."

He explained the situation to her. Miriam listened with interest, but mentioned she would not visit the establishment in question with him. He promised he would write to her ahead of coming out and arrange a place for them to meet. He explained that this would only ever be at night, as during the day he was too busy. She didn't question this.

"So, what are we meant to do about it?" she asked at the end.

"For now? No clue. Keep an eye out for the man, maybe ask around about him. He's pretty distinctive."

She laughed. "Will do. I should get ready to sleep soon. I have work tomorrow and I should get some more firewood. I didn't realise I had so little."

"I could get it for you." She was about to object, so he added, "Where is your purse?"

She blushed. "I'll get it myself. I don't need handouts."

"It's a business expense now. We just discussed the case."

"Is that right?" she asked, suspiciously.

"That's how it works." He stood to leave, and put a handful of coins on the table.

"That's too much."

"Excuse me. I get to decide that, don't I?"

She frowned, but thanked him, so he left.

He strolled out, but was stopped by Nettie. The old woman was still knitting outside her door; she must have developed the habit as the hall lights were brighter. "Come over here, young man."

He paused obediently. She was looking rather severe. "Madam?"

"I'd like to know what your intentions are towards my dear Miriam. She's got no family, but that doesn't mean she isn't cared for."

Sinjen softened towards her at once. "I like her. I'd like to be her friend."

She rolled a sherbet lemon in her mouth. "Well, I think you look like trouble."

"I do?" he asked. People usually said he looked very proper.

"Yes, in fact, I think you are a bad egg."

"Why?"

"You haven't even offered an old lady a place to sit," she insisted.

"But you are sitt—*Oh*."

She let out an amused cackle.

"Very well. When you put it like that, why not?"

By the time Nettie dismissed him, Sinjen very strongly suspected that what Miriam had told him about her was true. Nettie's rooms were filled with all manner of ornaments. Paintings, flowers and other gift items, like chocolate and perfume. She'd also turned to him, the moment he'd gone inside, with the most predatory expression he'd ever seen on a human female.

He assumed he'd been satisfactory, as she'd given him a bag of boiled sweets.

Henry tapped him on the shoulder as he exited the building. "You really do have the strangest taste in women," he sighed.

"Look, she might be ten years younger than me, but that's not too much."

He rolled his eyes. "You're robbing the cradle and the grave at once. Now you say it, though, I remember missing my generation when I got to about your age. I suppose it's fair enough."

"I recommend her, actually. That was terrifying, but in a good way."

Henry burst out laughing. "What's her story?"

"The widow of a vicar. Guess she went a little wild after he passed away."

"Well, she must have been good. You didn't even notice your girl leaving."

"She'll have gone to buy firewood, I think," Sinjen said, as they walked back to the brothel. "I suppose I should check on Jack."

They walked out the way Sinjen had arrived. Without warning, Harry took his shoulder and spirited them to the roof overlooking the alley they'd been passing. His expression was serious, so clearly they were hunting. Harry pointed down to the street below and Sinjen saw at once what it was.

Two men were down there. One all in black, wearing an ill-fitting overcoat in a dated style. The other blond, with a fur collar. They were fighting with real savagery, but neither called for help.

LIKE FATHER LIKE SON

The blond looked like he was winning, until the other picked up a broken wooden board and cracked him across the head with it. He was disoriented for long enough that the dark figure was able to seize him by the throat, pull his head to one side, and sink in his fangs. Harry was about to say something, but Sinjen raised a hand to stop him. The blond rallied and pulled a dirk from his coat, managing to plunge it through the vampire's ribcage with surprising force.

The man in black pulled back, clutching his side, and spirited away. The blond in the fur collar swayed on his feet, trying to stagger to safety. He only made it a few steps before he became too dizzy and had to press against the wall, barely clinging to consciousness.

"Harry, see if you can follow that vampire. Find out who he was."

Harry patted him on the backside, but nodded and vanished.

Jumping into the alley, Sinjen went over to the man. He stood behind him and supported him in his arms. He wasn't sure how he was still standing, his pulse was weak and too fast. He'd lost enough blood to kill him.

Sinjen stroked the scars across his cheek. They would have been deep enough to mark the bone, and the ones on his neck would have been almost fatal. Sinjen couldn't guess how he'd survived. Vampire hunters from hereditary clans were something else.

"Don't let me die. I know what you are, but this is personal. I can't die before he does. He'll kill my wife and son. Please." His voice was weak and he fell back against Sinjen's chest, no longer able to see.

Sinjen kissed his cheek. "You said the magic words." He tilted the man's head, and bit his neck. Trapping the man between his body and the wall, he had to adjust himself to support his weight as he weakened and died.

He looked up when he was done, in time to see Miriam staring at him, firewood and kindling in her arms, her face a mask of shock. When she saw that he'd seen her, she turned back to the street and hurried away.

Truth or Death

Chapter 7

"That's bad luck," Harry said with a grin, having watched from the roof for a time and seen Miriam flee.

Sinjen was still holding the blond man. It was painful; his soft leather jacket was embroidered all over with sacred symbols. It was pretty, though, well-crafted, insulated and made from lightly dyed suede. Sinjen started to remove it from his body, then spirited to the roof with him to finish removing any items that might damage him if he returned.

"You tried to turn him?" Harry asked. "They'll kill you both on the spot if they find out you turned a vampire hunter. Someone else could, perhaps, but not you. They'll think he's a risk."

"Yes," Sinjen agreed, "Fortunately, that rogue turned him. I assume you didn't find whoever he is? And he'll have nothing to do with me at all. You'll have to mind the fledgling, keep him alive for me."

"And why should I do that?" Harry asked, turning the man's face in his hands. "Hmm... I suppose he actually would be decent-looking as a vampire. Nobody would see the claw marks."

"Exactly. Who's going to know?"

"Suppose someone recognises him?"

"Then it'll be his own fault for letting his targets escape. Could you move him for me? We have two options: you could try and shove him into a locked beach hut, or there's a coffin lying around, up towards St. Mary's."

"Oh, that sounds fun. Leave the naked stiff in a box, dump the real body off a cliff. Sounds good, I'll do that. How *much* are you taking off him?"

"It's ridiculous, even his undergarments are embroidered." Sinjen sighed.

"To deter vampiresses, I bet. Amazing body, though, I can see why he'd need a magic union suit. So, what are you going to do?" Harry laughed.

"I'll have to go and kill Miriam, won't I?"

Harry raised an eyebrow. "That might not be necessary. You do have options..."

"Like what?"

"Well, from her expression, I don't think she thought you were killing him. I think she saw two men in a dark alley, one pressing the other against a wall from behind, and thought—"

"Oh, God. That would be harder to explain," Sinjen said, rubbing his forehead.

Harry laughed. "Exactly. So, you could just tell her the truth?"

"That it was murder?"

"That you're a vampire. You're a bit dense tonight, aren't you?"

"It's illeg—"

"Yeah, so? Everyone is doing it at the moment. I know Carlotta did. I have, but, well, it didn't work out that well for me. I had to finish her faster."

"Oh, you didn't turn her?"

"No, she had buck teeth. Really nice arse, though."

Sinjen rolled his eyes.

"Anyway, point is, it's what you wanted, wasn't it? A nice girl to revive you? How's she going to do that when she doesn't know who you are? Even you'll end up confused."

Sinjen leant back and took a deep breath. Harry picked up the body and threw it over his shoulder. Harry's own figure was wonderful. Moonlight wasn't a weak clan, and its knights were all rather impressive. "Maybe he can join Moonlight?"

"Yeah, don't worry about it, I'll look after your little boy, but I am doing this so you'll set me up with Carlotta, you know that? Though... he's not actually that little. I'm going to go now; this is too much naked man for my taste."

Sinjen snorted. He'd keep his clothes and knife safe for him, but that poor chap wouldn't have a strip of fabric on him when he woke up. If he awakened at all.

He lay on the roof for a little bit, wondering how he'd deal with Miriam. He'd be best off going to her with a gift, but she seemed choosy. He couldn't really put it off, as he didn't know when he'd be allowed out again.

Sinjen went to the main shopping street and found a shop selling ornaments. He browsed the shelves for a little while. There were some useful but expensive items. Some ceramic collectables, some Wedgwood, a few gold brooches and trinkets, which were rather pretty. He didn't know if Miriam didn't like jewellery, or if she'd just pawned whatever she might have had. She also might be upset with a gift that was too valuable.

His eye fell across a pair of statuettes: a fair young man chasing a pretty dark-haired girl who, turned away from him, had her eyes on the book in her hands. If she was turned towards him, it would look more like she was reading to him, or that he was trying to distract her from her story. It was also quite valuable, but she wouldn't necessarily know. He bought them from the surly shopkeeper and took them away in a box full of crumpled paper.

He spirited to her apartment and went in. Nettie was outside again. "Back for another tup?" she called.

"Woman, please, I can only take so much. But, no, I've already upset Miriam."

"That was fast," she laughed.

When he knocked on the door, Miriam answered right away, but her face fell at the sight of him. She sighed and let him in anyway.

"Before you say anything, just don't. I already had a lover who turned out to be a..."

"A... what?"

"A whoopsie, alright! I won't report you or anything, but don't waste my time." She turned around to see Sinjen laughing into his sleeve. "Why are you laughing?"

"I'm sorry, whoopsie is just such a funny term. I'm not one, not... well, you saw something else. I wanted a chance to explain. That's all."

She frowned at him and let him hand her the box. She peeked inside and smiled, but only put it on the table.

He went over and threw a few more logs onto her fire, noting that she did her best to hide the irritation she felt.

He spoke. "Listen, I can't do anything except waste your time. I can't marry you, or give you children." He tried not to look too amused as she turned scarlet.

"Then why are you here?"

"Because I like you. Also, I'm a vampire. I was killing the man you saw. He was a vampire hunter, though, in all fairness."

"Great. So you're completely insane. Get out."

"I am a vampire, I swear. Test me. Do you have a crucifix?"

"No. I have a Bible, though, why? Wait, why am I asking? Just leave."

"In a bit, if I can't prove it to you, then I'll leave you in peace, I promise. Go and get your Bible, hold it against my hand."

She rolled her eyes, but did so. "You know, when this doesn't do anything, could you please consider going to a hospital and letting them look you over?"

"Of course, darling," he said.

He put his hand on the table and she pressed the book over it. She'd expected some dramatics. Him to throw himself onto the ground, or scream, or cry, but he only stared at her, the pain in his eyes increasing, until eventually he sighed, "Please, that's enough. Look at what has happened."

She pulled it off and gasped, horrified at the sight of his burnt hand, red and almost skinless. "No, that can't be," she said, and fainted.

Sinjen caught her and carried her to her bed. He put the ornaments on her mantelpiece, then took her curtains off their poles. The fabric was threadbare and repaired in several places.

He spirited to a clothes shop. He knew it already, because it stayed open at all hours, being run from the home of a family of tailors. "Can you replace all of these in an hour with something nicer?" he asked.

The lady of the house looked at them, lifting a tattered corner and regarding it dismally. "Naturally. I have the perfect fabric, very popular. Would thick blue silk be alright? I can't do the frill on the edge in that time, but they will block out light instead of... whatever these do."

"That sounds perfect." He smiled and left the old ones with her. He sought a quiet spot and spirited to Jack.

Jack was lying on his bed, shirtless and asleep. A bandaged, jagged cut snaked from his neck down towards his heart. Sinjen could see the outline of the injury from the bloodstains. He rapped on the bed frame, and Jack opened his eyes.

"My word," Sinjen sighed. "I had no idea it had been so bad or I'd have come sooner."

Jack smiled. "I'm alright, really. It's Archie they're afraid for. If the bleeding doesn't stop, he's a goner. They've stitched it, but..."

"I'll do what I can," Sinjen said, sitting on his bed. He peeled off Jack's bandages, though Jack grabbed his hand and tried to stop him.

"You can't, I need those." There was something about his manner that suggested he'd been sedated. Jack was more relaxed and unfocused than he should have been.

"No, trust me." Sinjen uncovered the wound, and licked the cuts.

Jack shivered, then cried, "It'll get infected, are you mad?"

"No, it won't. It'll only stop the bleeding, I promise you." He waved his hand and compelled Jack to believe him. "I want you to work for me. You'll never be able to fully leave my service, but I want you to be mine. Be my thrall, I'll be your master. Can you understand me? I'm not human, but a vampire. The truth is, I need others to survive, including their service. I won't hurt you."

Jack stroked his hair and drew him in for a kiss. "Alright, but only if you'll look after my sister and save Archie. I'd say get her out of this life, but she's good at it, and good with the girls. They'd suffer without her."

"Okay. You can ask for whatever you'd like, I don't mind at all. When we make our agreement, I'll have to honour whatever you ask. The exception being to turn you. At best I can only try – it's not in my hands, ultimately."

"God's hands?" he asked, drawing him close. Sinjen embraced him.

"Yes. I can only curse who he allows, but at least I can choose my own company. Please, be with me."

Jack kissed his cheek. "I'd like that. Go and save Archie and I'm yours."

Sinjen left. He compelled Archie to sleep the minute he entered the room, and licked his wounds until they healed, some even closing over. He added a hypnotic suggestion that Archie would recover well and resist infection, but he could only do his best. A few major arteries had been severed, and though he'd tried, he could only help. He did taste better than Jack; he probably led a more sensible life. He inspected the man's face. He was burly and angular, the corners of his lips tended upwards and he had smile lines around his eyes. He seemed pleasant enough.

Sinjen returned to the dressmakers, collected the curtains and replaced them. By the time Miriam woke, he was immersed in an absurd romance about a woman who'd run away to become a pirate, and the woman she'd fallen for. He was just wondering if he knew her, when Miriam coughed.

"My curtains? Show me your hand." He showed her. It had long healed. "Then I dreamt it. I must have."

"Want me to show you more?" he asked.

She burst into tears. "I lied before. My father had a heart attack and then my mother jumped from the cliffs. I was so angry and frightened, but, there's no way. They say that suicides can become... like you."

"Well, if she is, I don't know her," he said, having unintentionally reverted to his cold aspect.

"I'm sorry. I didn't mean to suggest... How did you... end up that way?"

"I was turned directly, by a vampiress who wanted me. My maker and her family are dead. I don't want to talk about it. Now, my 'aunt', who is not my aunt, keeps me prisoner instead. A vampiric princess, as mad as we come."

"You really are a monster?"

"I... I don't want to be, but yes."

She cried. After a little while he went over and held her. She put her arms around him and asked, "Show me more."

He smiled and kissed her cheek.

Sinjen spirited them to the roof of her building. She clung to him for dear life, but was not sick. She'd tolerated it without suffering. He thought she'd turn well. "I'll take you anywhere you can see. Choose a place."

She surveyed the scene for a little while. "Up there. On the top, above everyone." She pointed to where she wanted and Sinjen grinned. He kissed her, and then they were at Whitby Abbey, atop the thick stone walls. He held her tightly, more than a little afraid that she would fall.

"Is it okay?" he asked.

"It's magnificent," she breathed. "But there, that's where my mother... it's where she jumped."

Sinjen looked towards the cliffs. "You're still so young to be without your parents. Mine passed away when I was young too. I'm really sorry."

"What happened to yours?" she asked.

"I don't know, exactly. The doctors said it was typhoid fever. I was never certain. They'd been away, and I thought, perhaps, spoiled food on the journey. I don't know."

"I'm sorry. How old are you?"

He laughed, "Young for a vampire. I've been one for fifty years, I was born in 1812."

"My God, then you'll be eighty-eight?"

"Goodness. Will I?"

She actually laughed. "What does that feel like?"

"Hmm. I haven't changed physically, but I feel like I've missed out on so much. I feel..." He thought for a few moments. "I feel like there's nothing left of me, like I'm out of my own time. But also – because of the lights and the new things, and because I finally have a little freedom – I want to live again, properly, not just survive."

"That's pretty." Miriam sighed. "I wish I was so strong."

He chuckled. "You are. Do you want to see my fangs?"

She touched his face, he parted his lips, and she ran her thumb along his teeth to look. He extended his fangs and felt her touch the elongated canines. It was more difficult than he'd expected not to bite the soft pad of her thumb. He sighed as she let him go. "Lie down."

"I can't, that's— We're in public."

He laughed. "It's late, and people don't look up as much as you might think they do. It's alright. I won't let you come to harm."

She sighed, kissed him and let him push her down onto the wall of the cathedral. The whole thing was a roofless ruin, but the walls were thick enough. They embraced, and he felt her pull him closer when a cold wind blew. He put his hand up her skirt, sliding it up to the edge of her corset as he kissed her, then down again between her legs.

"Don't!" she cried. He felt her writhe beneath him, but it wouldn't have been right for either of them.

"Okay," he said, and kissed her deeply again. "I'll take you home."

Taking Care of a Loose End

Chapter 8

H arry met him watching the sea. Sinjen wasn't sure where he'd gone, but figured he'd turn up if he stayed somewhere obvious. He showed up with a few bottles of port, some kippers and a box of cigars in a mesh bag. He'd slung them all over his shoulder.

"Kippers?" Sinjen asked.

"I like kippers. You can't really get them in Italy."

"Are you from England, then?"

"My estate was in Kent, but I've always loved Italy. It's the clothes and the climate," Harry said, smiling.

"We have excellent tailors here," Sinjen's patriotism compelled him to point out.

"Yes, and I'll visit them, but I like my clothes a bit flashier. So, tell me, how do I get Carlotta to spend time with me? She's not far from us, and I want to make the most of it."

"Did you come here just for her?" Sinjen asked.

"Alright, maybe I did. I just woke up one morning and realised, even though I've loved her for years, I'd never acted on it. A lifetime had already slipped away."

"I suppose that happens more quickly if you spend decades in an opium den." Sinjen sighed.

"How on earth did you know that? But, yes, that's a factor."

"You forgot, perhaps. We were sent to the same cull. You because you smoked too much of Blackthorn's product." He could only imagine Harry had still been in a bit of a haze at the time.

"Oh, well, to be fair, I gave most of it to my friends. It's the easiest way to hunt – mostly napping, endless new people, and if one of them dies nobody thinks anything of it. I suppose I just needed a rest... I don't remember you being at the cull," Harry admitted, rubbing his neck.

"Really? I kicked you into a group of vampire hunters so I could escape. I've been at every one that's happened since I was made."

"Oh. That rings a bell, but never mind. You're a bit young to have stood a chance without some ruthlessness, I suppose."

Sinjen smiled softly, and they watched the sea in silence for a little while. He had been aware that Harry was popular, but for someone with such a reputation for being difficult and callous, he really wasn't what he'd expected.

"She wants to learn to ride a bicycle, but she's a bit shy about doing it on her own. She's got riding clothes and everything. Why don't you offer to teach her?"

"And see her in bloomers?" Harry grinned. "Sounds good. You know, you aren't the person I thought you were. Everyone says you're a monster, and you are, I guess, but you're so different away from Eliza."

Sinjen's smile faltered for a fraction of a second. "Let's get oysters and champagne, and then we should go back." He wouldn't be able to see Miriam again, perhaps for weeks – there was no way his little taste of freedom would last.

The second they entered the house, Harry noticed that Sinjen's face had reverted to his usual unpleasant mask. He thought he must be anticipating something bad, too, as he'd smoked three cigarettes on his way back. They both bowed when Eliza strode into the room. Sinjen followed her out; she hadn't needed to give him more than a look.

"I'm going away tomorrow, Sinjen. You can help me tie up loose ends," she demanded. The usual chill ran through him. A statement like that could mean anything from 'run errands for me', to 'I'll need to brick you into a wall and leave you there until I want you back.'

She led him up to her bedroom. He could see from the way the servants were hurrying about that she'd been busy. The absolute terror on their faces as they tried to clean up, while keeping out of sight, indicated that she'd been finishing off her last collection of girls and possibly one or two of the staff. He kept his face neutral. Her father must have called her home. He and Margaret would likely return too. Nightfall Castle was horrific. Nothing good ever happened to him there; his mood grew very dark.

He followed her into her room. He'd been in smaller ballrooms. By sight it was alarmingly normal, even luxurious and elegant, her paraphernalia concealed in purpose-built storage. Only the metal in the ceilings might seem strange. She hadn't used this room earlier, or there would still be bloodstains. He would have sighed if it was safe – he'd spotted the loose end.

Laura was sitting at the end of Eliza's bed, as still as a statue. The poor thing would be terrified, but she smiled as Eliza entered.

"I asked the girl, since she's been good, if she had a last request, and guess what it was?" Eliza said, turning to Sinjen.

He grinned. "Let me think, to spend eternity with you?"

Eliza laughed. "Nothing even so grand. She only wanted you to do it, isn't that just darling?"

He was shocked, and had to look away for a moment to collect himself.

"If *you* kill me, Sinjen, then I don't think I'll mind," Laura said, her voice quavering. Poor girl. She must have felt like all she could do was buy a few more hours.

"So, what shall we do about her?" Eliza said, with a grin.

"Do I have to be rough?"

She laughed. "No, I suppose I've had enough of that for today. Just amuse me."

He embraced Eliza, and breathed in the scent of her hair. She'd put it up, but it was still damp and smelled metallic. He could see a trail of dried, watered-down blood, running from the nape of her neck to her collar. He traced it and felt her shiver. He hated that both of those things had aroused him and took a deep breath, remembering that it was necessary, however he felt about it.

Eliza hadn't bothered to dress again, in her elaborate way, and instead wore a tea gown, burgundy with black lace. Chains of black pearls gleamed where they hung from her neck and wrists. He kissed her, and brushed a lock of hair behind her ear. At least she was already in a good mood. Laura hadn't been foolish; she might get a painless death. It was just a shame that her efforts wouldn't save her when she'd tried so hard.

Sinjen took Eliza's hand and brought her over to the bed. The pair began to undress Laura. When Sinjen cupped Laura's breast she gasped and leant against him. Her hand reached for his, and she interlaced their fingers. Sinjen was visibly surprised and wrapped his other arm around her waist. She smiled, then gasped, as Eliza slid her hand up her leg. Laura turned her head and kissed him full on the lips. He recoiled and looked to Eliza, who was grinning.

"What's the matter, Sinjen? Didn't you notice that she was in love with you?"

"I didn't, Lady Eliza. I'm not in the habit of looking at other women, not when you're around."

Eliza scowled. He'd misspoken – she knew the kinds of things Sinjen got up to when she wasn't there.

When they had amused themselves enough, Sinjen asked Eliza to help him drain her. He'd already fed from the vampire hunter that night, but she too was full.

She sent for Harry, who bit Laura first, then was dismissed. He showed no reaction to the scene, the naked girl leaning against Sinjen's bare chest and Eliza hardly dressed. Harry remembered to kiss Eliza's hand before he left.

Sinjen finished her off. His hands shook, though Laura held them against her chest until she lost consciousness.

Eliza laughed. "You monster. I'd have let you keep her, but you can't tolerate competition, can you?"

He looked up, horrified. "I thought this was what you wanted?"

She took him by the hair and bit his shoulder, not to drain him, just to hurt. He reached out by instinct, trying to push her off. She caught his arms, and struck him hard enough to knock him off the bed. A vampire her age was practically indestructible.

"Did you just raise a hand to me?" she hissed.

"I-I was afraid, I didn't mean to. I'm sorry, Mistress. Did I hurt you?" he cried, abject desperation in his voice.

She looked down her nose at him, retied her dress, then took him by his hair and dragged him towards a large empty wardrobe. She instructed him to get in and to stay, then went to the bed and dragged Laura over too. She threw the girl's body on top of him and locked the doors.

"Stay there and think about what you've done," she commanded, and went to make sure Margaret had packed.

Sinjen sighed once she had gone. This bloody wardrobe again – not normal furniture, but one designed to hold vampires and humans alike. The insides were carved with sacred symbols that stung on contact. He had no clothes on and neither did Laura, but he took care to hold her so that her body would not touch the lined walls. He'd taken a gamble. He hadn't been certain whether Eliza had wanted Laura, and had decided to try to turn her without permission. If she awoke, he could always have tried to pass it off as an accident, but trying to create two vampires in a night, especially his first two, wasn't a sure thing.

He fell asleep, or rested as well as he could, with the symbols burning into his back. At least it would be dawn soon and he'd be unconscious of the pain.

He awoke the next night to Laura kissing his lips and chest. "I knew you'd help me," she whispered, "I knew you would."

He laughed very quietly. "I didn't even know that," he said, and put his finger against her lips. He could hear Eliza stirring. She walked over and opened the wardrobe, impassively regarding Laura straddling Sinjen's lap and smiling up at her. Sinjen's expression was pained; his back was red, the symbols scorched into his skin.

"So. I have two of you now. That's *nice*. Get dressed and feed the girl," Eliza said.

Sinjen took Laura by the hand and walked them both to his room. He dressed, and sent a maid to bring clothes for Laura. Afterwards, he hypnotised the young woman and instructed Laura to kill her. "No point wasting time. Just feed, and we'll see what Lady Eliza has planned."

As he finished helping Laura dress, Eliza returned again.

"Margaret and I are ready to leave. I'm going to take Laura with me. I want you to stay and mind the house. I should be away for a week or two."

Sinjen was so shocked that his knees buckled. Laura had to steady him, then Eliza sent her to pack. He hoped that she would have an easier time with Eliza than he had. It was possible – she was sometimes affectionate to women.

"You really trust me to be alone?" he asked, unable to believe his luck.

"You've spent, what, twenty-five years in my service without major incident? I'm sure you can manage a week or two without me."

He couldn't help it, and went over to his bed to sit down. She grinned at his disbelief.

"There's something you should know. You have to grow up a bit now, I'm getting a bit bored of the simpering. Work on your own reputation, and be less dull. Do as you please when I go. I expect a few scandals," she instructed, and stormed out.

He was left sitting with his hand over his mouth, staring at the door.

He went to see them off when they were ready, and gave Margaret the bag of sherbet lemons for the trip. She grinned, but was already chewing a liquorish root, and hugged him before hopping into the carriage.

Eliza pulled a lock of his hair, hard, but otherwise ignored him.

"Goodbye my darlings, have a safe trip," he called with genuine affection.

"Bye, Sinjen!" Margaret cried in return. Eliza only sighed and shut the carriage window.

He watched them drive away, then went back indoors in a daze. There were still a few vampires staying with them, including Carlotta, so he went to her room. Predictably, Harry was there. He was sitting with her at the window, while she read the latest issue of *Vogue*. Sinjen walked straight up to Carlotta, put his arms around her waist and began to cry with relief, hiding his face in her skirts. She didn't say anything, but stroked his hair.

When he'd calmed down, Harry patted him on the shoulder. "Holy shit, you're a good actor. I thought you were in love with her."

"I hope she falls into a charcoal oven," Sinjen said, as Carlotta smacked him on the back of the head.

"It's still not safe to say things like that," she cautioned.

Sinjen half-laughed, half-cried. Before he knew it, he was letting Harry pour him a large whiskey and press a cigar into his hand.

Nostalgia

Chapter 9

Eliza had put him through any number of torments, but last night's ordeal with Laura had left him with more self-disgust than he had harboured in a long while. Sinjen checked his back, and thought the marks would fade by about midnight. Burns and injuries by holy objects generally took the longest to heal, but he did recover a little faster than usual from the latter, perhaps because his maker had been from Daylight and they had had strong resistances. If his original clan had lived, he could have looked forward to becoming a day walker in just over a decade. The loss of that hope had been its own type of grief.

He took a bath and collected his thoughts, before writing to meet Miriam the next night and going to find Harry. Carlotta had already dismissed him and gone out with her friends, Meghan Nightingale and Tansy Darkwood. Tansy was a higher-up with Tigers-Eye, who did a lot of the coordination between branches. He hadn't seen much of her, but she was elegant, willowy and rather frightening, according to rumour. She didn't seem it, though; she seemed wise and reassuring.

Tansy was a striking beauty with long black hair and delicate freckled skin so fair it could seem translucent. Meghan was an inquisitor, but not the worst one to deal with, strong and fair-minded.

Harry was pacing in his room.

"I'm thinking of throwing a pool party, what do you think? I keep hearing about these new swimsuits, but I haven't actually seen one yet," Sinjen said.

"You know, neither have I, except for in the newspaper. I approve." He brightened up, so Sinjen asked if he would take him out for a drive.

"I'd like to see someone I used to know. I think she's still kicking."

Harry raised an eyebrow, "You can't talk to her."

"No, she'd die of fright, but I want to look at her. It's been so long."

He sighed, "You're going to upset yourself, but alright. Let's go."

Harry pulled up to the village near the Northern estate. "So, what's the story?" he asked.

"This is my cousin's place. I'll invite you in, but I don't want anyone harmed, this is family." Harry grinned, but agreed. Sinjen had been invited, long ago, by letter. They spirited to the edge of the grounds, then Sinjen jumped the wall and called Harry in. He climbed over and followed Sinjen through the gardens to a spot with a view of the house.

"A big chunk of this burned down, but I guess they fixed it in the end," Sinjen whispered. "You can still see some smoke stains though, on the stone – look."

"Charming. So, we're looking for some cute granny?"

"No, she'll be a serious and plain granny, likely in the most simple clothing you've ever seen."

Harry chuckled. "This is who Miriam reminds you of, then?"

"See the light? Let's go to the balcony, up there." They spirited up and peered through the latticed windows. They saw a little old woman reading in her bed. She was dressed in a black nightdress with white lace on the sleeves and a white nightcap.

A much younger woman, who resembled her, brought in a herbal tea and placed it at her bedside. She had brown hair, sleek and compliant with the neat style she wore. It was much like his cousin had worn it at that age. In their youth, her discipline had attracted him. If she had held the same sway over her wilful heart, they might have married.

It was strange to think of now, after decades without real love, but back then he'd been so certain that she was wrong. The two women spoke for a little while, with affectionate expressions and voices as gentle and soft-spoken as his own. His cousin smiled more than she had in her younger years. Sinjen did start to get a bit emotional, as Harry had predicted.

"Did she look like – that must be her granddaughter – when she was young?" Harry whispered.

"She's much more beautiful," Sinjen admitted. "My cousin was more mousy and serious, but they aren't dissimilar. Actually, I'm quite impressed by the granddaughter."

"There's just something about third cousins, I swear. She looks decent enough to me, but I don't see what's so impressive," Harry contributed.

"I suppose, in theory, I could marry her and inherit my own family's holdings? Though she might have a brother. If so..."

"Why not? I did. Frittered away our family fortune more than once."

"My God, did you really?"

Harry laughed. "No, just kidding. I murdered my family before I'd even died."

Sinjen stared at him, then glanced back at the window. They both vanished at once. The old lady had gotten up to open the latch, and accidentally caught a great view of Sinjen. He and Harry retreated to the roof above her.

They heard her open the window and ask, "Cousin? My goodness. What *is* the matter with me?"

Her granddaughter rushed back in and helped her back into bed. Sinjen dropped below the window again and listened as the old woman explained that she thought for a moment, she'd seen her "dear cousin". She over-generously surmised his life and character to the younger woman. Sinjen and Harry listened a little longer, then spirited back to the nearby woods.

Sinjen was lost in his own reflections and Harry guided him back to the car, before clapping him on the back and suggesting that they go to the nearest town to get tanked. Sinjen laughed and agreed.

Harry, when they arrived in Harrogate, asked around and found a likely place. Another brothel, but this one catered to the very wealthy. This, Sinjen assumed, meant that he was paying for them.

The next thing he knew, he was waking up in a wooden box.

He spirited out, and searched around for his companion. He found his car first, and Harry joined him a bit later. "What the hell happened?" he asked.

"You said you were paying." Harry laughed.

Sinjen rolled his eyes and neatened his suit. "Okay, lesson learnt. You just shoved me in a box?"

"Well, I wasn't going to carry you around all night, was I? Don't you remember any of it?"

They got in the car, and Harry recounted what he recalled.

"Okay. I don't believe any of that, but can you tell people that all of those things happened."

"It did happen, but I guess you were in a funny mood to start with. At one point, you had everyone making so much noise that the police turned up, so you hypnotised them into joining in. Pretty sure you got at least three of them into bed."

"Did I?"

"Yes, but I don't remember much of what happened after we left."

"So, where did you sleep?" Sinjen asked.

"Some woman's house. Do you still have all your things?"

"Most of them." He sighed. "I said I'd meet Miriam tonight. Want to come?"

"Yes, actually. I was thinking of taking a mistress. There's quite a beautiful girl in the next brothel over, and she's already rather delicate. I can't stop thinking about her."

"I see," Sinjen said, frowning. "Why do you do that, anyway?"

"I'll tell you someday, when I know you better," Harry promised.

Harry cleared off when they got to Whitby. Sinjen assumed that this was a sign of trust, but wasn't dumb enough to believe there was no possibility that he was being watched. He'd said he'd meet Miriam at the tea house, but went to her room first and topped up her coin purse. Seeing that she still hadn't bothered adjusting her standards and buying more fuel, he bought her a full bucket of coal and another bag of logs. On a whim, he also got a pretty rug. Anything to make her room a little more comfortable. He suspected he'd get in trouble for it, but went to meet her.

She looked angry when he came in, but he thought it might be her book. He greeted her a little cautiously.

"Do you know why I'm angry?" she asked.

Sinjen could think of a few potential reasons, but wasn't willing to volunteer one in case his answer was incorrect. Instead he turned around and ordered some black tea and slices of a sponge cake with pink, rose-scented icing. Then he sat down and waited for her to tell him. She just kept looking at him, hoping he'd cave.

"Can you give me a clue?" he asked.

"It's about where I work."

"Oh, good. I don't have the slightest idea. You never told me where you work."

She sighed. "I do the books for a few different shops. But you see, there was a break in at the dress shop and I thought it seemed rather odd. It happened last night, but nobody has touched it yet. The owners are away for a little while, now that the holidays are done, because it's quiet in January. I was called to deal with it and have only locked the shop for now. Do you want to take a look?"

"I do," he said, smiling at her.

She frowned at him. "And the money you left..."

"Just keep it. If I told you what I spent last night, on less worthy causes, you'd consider it a public service. And I'm sorry I was late; it was a long drive tonight." It had been a long way, even if Harry drove like a madman.

"Is that right?"

He noticed that she'd at least bought new gloves, and the string on her pince-nez had been replaced by a black beaded chain. It was rather pretty, sparkling as she ate. He resisted the urge to count the little beads, but did estimate their number.

"Why are you smiling like that?" she asked.

"You look pretty. Your colour looks nicer, I think, and your hair... is it different?"

She blushed a little. "I went to a hairdresser. It's been nice, actually, to have a little to spend on niceties. If I were a man I'd be on a respectable wage, but I'm not paid what I'm worth. Even if I do reading and letter-writing on the side." She sighed. "Sometimes it's a little bit frustrating. There are less difficult ways to make better money around here. Occasionally, I think I'd have a decent chance of finding a husband if I did them. I wouldn't, of course, but I'm not actually unaware of that truth."

"You want to get married?"

"Nettie thinks I'm going to end up as an old maid. She says I'm too sober and not the kind of woman a man wants."

"You're exactly the kind of woman I would have wanted, when I was young," he told her.

"Well, great, but it might as well be my grandfather telling me so."

He raised his eyebrows, hurt enough that she apologised.

"I didn't mean that the way it sounded. I meant we aren't the same generation. It does feel like men now are more interested in fleeting pleasures, diversions. That kind of thing..."

"Nettie *is* quite fun." She kicked him lightly under the table, and he laughed, "Let's go and see this shop then."

The streets of Whitby had a tendency to be a little winding; even the buildings looked a bit jaunty. The second storeys had a tendency to overhang, or else the shop signs contributed to the impression that they did. Colourful rows of bunting were strung from one side of the road to the other in a few places, and flickered in the sea breeze.

He spotted Harry as they walked across town; he was contemplating a jewellers window. Sinjen tapped him on the shoulder as they passed, and motioned for him to come too.

"Who is he?" Miriam asked.

"Another like me. This is Henry Balcom. It's okay, we're friends," Sinjen assured her.

She looked at them, taking in Sinjen's neat step and carefully calculated clothing and demeanour, then Harry's flashy suit, his amused grin and easy manner. She couldn't help noticing the sound as his shiny shoes tapped buoyantly against the cobblestones. Next to one another, Sinjen appeared more unsettling. He seemed deceptively perfect, while Harry's manner, against Sinjen's, came across as reckless and without care.

In spite of that, there was something in Harry's eyes which suggested an unnatural intelligence, smart enough to appear more foolish than he was, perhaps. She could see he was keenly astute when it came to other people. Even now he was watching her while pretending not to.

"You two are friends?" she asked.

Harry winked at her, "You must be Miss Green. Sinjen's been telling me all about you, he's been rather infatuated."

"And how old are you?"

"I don't know. Two hundred and fifty? I was a young man during the Restoration."

"Oh," she said, and held Sinjen's elbow, feeling a sudden urge to find safety. He smiled and kissed her lightly on the cheek.

Sand on the Floor

Chapter 10

"Well, I guess I'll show you what I think," Miriam began, as she unlocked the shop for them. The door had been forced open, but she'd arranged for it to be chained and bolted until the original mechanism could be replaced. "The shopkeeper next door discovered the break-in in the morning and sent for me, but it's a small wonder that nobody woke when the door was damaged. So, I guess whoever it was had a little experience. That's not the strangest thing, though – I'll show you."

Sinjen had a look around the establishment before he went inside. "I assume the curtains were down at the time?" he asked.

"Yes. This thief knew what they would find in here, I expect," Miriam said, watching him look around from the doorway. Harry was standing further back, looking around too, but more as though he were casing the street himself.

"I know this place," Harry offered. "They have some pretty nice clothes, but you have to arrange for it to be open at night."

"Look here, Sinjen," Miriam called, "this is the first strange thing."

She pointed to the floor, a little way in from the door. There were some cushioned footstools, where customers might wait while whoever they came with tried on clothes. There was only one changing room, but quite large, with heavy curtains and a long mirror. Sinjen spotted Miriam checking to see if he had a reflection and waved.

What Miriam had drawn his attention to, however, was a patch of sand. Miriam continued, "There was a crumpled outfit here when I reported it. Likely belonging to a fisherman from the smell and the fabric; faded and worn by sand, sun and sea. The police took it because they knew already to whom it belonged. They'd found the body of a man on the beach. They think he was night foraging, but he drowned and most of his clothes were stolen."

This shop was a little recessed from the promenade, not miles from the beach, but a little walk. Not a journey someone could make without any clothes on.

"They do sell budget, even second-hand options, as well as their more valuable items. Of course, they have to be nice quality. The second thing which is odd is that nothing else was touched. Only one full outfit was taken, and it was an expensive set of clothes – shoes too. Above the value you could get in real trouble over."

Harry and Sinjen exchanged a glance. "So, what do you think happened?" Sinjen asked.

Miriam frowned at him. "Well, what it seems is that someone came up from the beach, killed a man, leaving no marks on him, and came to a shop he might have browsed before. If I had to guess, I'd say someone

86

rich, and not likely a career criminal, because they'd know to take something less expensive. They would have taken more of the stock, if they had planned a robbery. I was wondering if either of you two might know why a wealthy man could have been staggering about with no clothes on last night?"

Harry poked Sinjen in the back of his shoulder. "Oh. Alright then, I can see why you like her," he whispered.

Sinjen cleared his throat. "It might happen that we have some idea."

"That vampire hunter?" Miriam asked.

"I suspect so," Sinjen admitted.

"These were men's clothes?" Harry asked.

"Yes, why?" Miriam said, going to the counter to fetch the shop's stock list.

"The other person it might have been was a woman. I thought I'd better ask, if they came up from the beach. Not so wealthy either, I think. Sinjen, how would he get down from St. Mary's in the buff?"

"Spirited perhaps?" he suggested. "Carlotta told me that when she first got out of her coffin she ended up in the woods, about a mile away from her grave, in her funerary clothes, barely dressed. She was terrified. I don't know who made her, but I'd like to knock them out."

"Oh, yes. She did tell me you hadn't wanted her turned."

Sinjen scowled at him. "It wasn't you, was it?"

"I was at Moonlight back then," Harry assured him. "I don't blame whoever she convinced, though. Be a hard heart that could refuse a woman that sweet and pretty, pleading to be changed."

"I'm sure it was a man." Sinjen sighed. "I was bloody furious. I don't know how she even found one of us. I certainly didn't let her meet anyone, except for Leo. He wouldn't have, though, I'm sure he wouldn't."

"Who's Carlotta?" Miriam asked, bringing over a note she'd been writing.

"My future wife," Harry said, rather wistfully.

"And a friend of mine when I was alive," Sinjen added, resisting the urge to glare at Harry.

"Yes, well, anyway. The items taken were: a grey dress coat, black trousers, a short black top hat, a white shirt and grey waistcoat, socks, black shoes and... um, you know, the rest. Did you leave him totally..."

"I'm afraid so," Sinjen said, rubbing his neck. "I didn't have a lot of time, and I had to speak to you too."

"I hope you plan on spending the night looking for him. I'm not wandering about the town alone trying to find him."

"Do you want to wander about with me?" Sinjen asked.

She sighed. "Okay, but..." she added, looking at the clothes, "maybe I should dress like someone else. I might run into someone I know."

Harry went back to the brothels, Sinjen reasoning that there was a fair chance their target would turn up back there.

Sinjen, on the other hand, had a small argument with Miriam over whether she should dress a class up, if or they should both dress down. Sinjen won in the end, claiming that it would be easier to bribe people if they looked like their money belonged to them.

He helped her pick out something appropriate and paid for it. She was unrecognisable. He pointed out that she wouldn't look too out of place in a top-class brothel, so she struck him with her new handbag.

"You do look beautiful, though. I bet if Carlotta were here, she could work wonders. Hair and makeup, I mean. I'm no use at all that."

Miriam fidgeted with her clothing, but, looking at her reflection, admitted to herself that she wasn't likely to be recognised. She put her glasses into the handbag, just in case she needed them for reading. Sinjen took her arm, and she blushed when she saw in the mirror that they made quite a pretty couple.

"I don't feel like myself at all. What on earth am I getting myself into?" she asked.

Sinjen smiled and gently kissed her lips. "I'll keep you safe, just as long as you're enjoying yourself."

"You're so certain you can keep me safe? There are two rogue vampires now, not only one."

"Yes, but there might be something sensible we can do tomorrow, if we can't find anyone tonight."

"You know, I can do things during the day too," she pointed out.

"You're welcome to," he said, but he shot her a nervous glance. "Our fledgling will need to feed again, and to find a place to sleep. He can always return to his grave. Though, perhaps, as he was buried in someone else's, maybe he can't. I'm not sure. He'll need a dark place to shelter."

Miriam looked thoughtful. "If it was me, and I didn't already live in Whitby... Did he?" Sinjen shook his head. "Then, I guess I'd try the holiday shacks on the hills. Some of them are half-buried. Should we check the cemetery first?"

"I think that's a good idea," he said, a little adoringly.

They walked up to the church again. Miriam was holding his arm, and Sinjen couldn't help looking at her. He did it so often that she told him off. There was a light drizzle and he was wondering if he should have gotten her a parasol or something. "I hope you keep those clothes, they suit you. But what's the matter? Surely I can look at you?"

She looked at the ground, "It's the way you're doing it. And..."

"Because I'm an awful bloodsucking creature of the night, condemned to walk the earth, feeding on the living to sustain my unholy existence?" he asked. She burst into tears, and he had to hold her. "It's not your fault, you know. What would you do? Put me out of my misery?"

"Would you want me to?" she asked, looking into his eyes with genuine pity and concern.

He took her hand and led her to the railings, overlooking the beach. "See there? If I wanted to die I could walk into the sea, or burn myself alive, or fall asleep in a field, far from safety. I could let someone I don't trust know where I sleep. I don't have to live any more than you do."

"Sinjen, you can't be telling me that you'd be willing to die a suicide."

His expression became too pained to hide for a moment. "I sleep... in the basement of a house I own. A cottage, five miles from here. Here's the key. My guardian is there, but if you go in, he won't stop you from harming me. Don't ask me foolish things. If I'm a monster in your eyes, then kill me."

"So you do want to die?" she asked.

He turned to her with contempt. It took him a second to repress the anger in his voice. "Maybe. I just don't think you'll kill your meal ticket."

She slapped him and started to walk home. He watched her go, leaning against the railings. When she'd gone far enough away that she'd have had to leave his sight to get home, she turned around, saw him still watching her and ran back to him. She put her arms around him and, though he was still annoyed, he let her.

"I was asking out of genuine concern. I couldn't love you and want you to be damned, it would be false."

He hadn't expected that, and put his hand on the back of her neck, another around her shoulders. "As I live, I am damned. I'm afraid. I led a good life, I thought. If I go after all I have done, as a monster, would I be damned for that instead? Can I tell myself it didn't count?"

"God will have mercy on you," she insisted.

"I can feel that I'm far from Him, but that's enough about this. Let's find the former vampire hunter and the rogue, if we can. You're a good woman. I know I can't be anything to you, but you'll marry, I'm sure."

She took his hand and dragged him up the hill.

Well-known Names

Chapter 11

The grave was undisturbed, and if he was presently in it, it wouldn't have been. It lacked a headstone, but a wooden cross bearing a woman's name had been pressed into the freshly levelled soil as a temporary marker. Sinjen had looked uncomfortable since they'd entered the churchyard.

"What now?" Miriam asked, looking around and up at the ruins. "We can't dig it up."

"I can take us to look at the shacks? I'd quite like to leave anyway. I'm not supposed to be here. Failing that, we could investigate the brothel, if you are curious to see it, or I could go there and find Harry. There is a man who keeps a list of known rogue vampires, too, but even the way Harry drives it would be almost impossible to reach him tonight. I don't suppose you fancy staying with the two of us, for a day and two nights?"

She frowned and fiddled with her glove. "I have the day after tomorrow off."

"Really? You'd come out with two vampires, just like that?"

"I can if I like, I suppose."

He held her hands and kissed her. He'd thought she would pull away, but instead she held him tightly. She hadn't given the key to the cottage back yet.

Sinjen spirited them to the roof of the brothel. The shacks were too far, and he needed to calm down.

"Are you alright?" she asked.

"Consecrated ground. It feels a bit like falling from a very high building; it's terrifying. May I have a drink?"

She laughed. "I wouldn't mind one myself, actually."

He spirited them back around the corner, and they walked in. Sinjen took her into the main building, where Harry was very much the centre of attention. He had the woman he'd mentioned at his side, even though she wasn't from this establishment. She and a few other girls, as well as a few male guests, were playing hazard.

Sinjen shook his head and steered Miriam to Carol, who was tending the bar.

She winked at them. "Good evening, Miriam. We've got ice-cream and wine."

Miriam flushed. "It's not what you think, I promise. I'd like a red, though."

"You two know each other?" Sinjen said, smiling. "A large whiskey, please. Don't worry, Miriam is just helping me look into the situation with Miss Webb."

Carol poured the drinks and asked, "You really are looking into that? I'm surprised, most people wouldn't."

"We are. It's been a bit fun. I thought Miriam should dress up a little, though. How do you know her?"

"She reads the newspapers to me. I like to keep informed."

Miriam would not meet his eye, and downed her drink too quickly. "It's more normal than I expected in here, kind of nice, actually."

"That's the idea," Carol assured her. "The less glamorous side of things doesn't happen here, after all. I do strongly advise you against considering this kind of work though, Miriam. I don't think it would do you any good."

She turned bright pink, almost matching her dress. "I don't, I mean, I'm not. Is Miss Webb still alright?"

"She's fine, but she's not here. She's staying with a friend now. She was quite shaken up."

They continued to talk, but Sinjen was hardly listening. He was looking around the establishment for any sign of either vampire. He went over to Harry and asked if he'd seen anything.

"Yep, there was one here earlier. The rogue," Harry responded without looking up from their game. "I was a bit absorbed, and didn't follow him, but he's changed clothes. Something better fitted, black with a red shirt. He had a cane and a top hat as well."

"Why didn't you follow him? Do you know who he is?" Sinjen asked.

"Hell, yes, I know who he is. That's why I didn't follow him."

"Care to divulge that information?"

"No. I'm not getting involved. Your new friend, and his boy, are already for it. Not yet, perhaps, but there's nothing to be done."

"I'm going to check on Jack. We'll talk about this later, though. Can you take us to see Lord Petri?"

Harry laughed, and shook his head. "I said I'm not getting involved, and there's very little point looking for clues with Petri – better off finding your friend. Think well-known names. Leave me alone now, I'm on a winning streak." Some of the women looked between Sinjen and Harry, puzzling over their conversation, but there was nothing really in it. Sinjen ignored the ones trying to get his attention and waved at Carol before leaving.

Jack was now much better. He was in the same room as before, having his injury tended by a pretty young woman with soft features. Everything about her was soft; she even smelled of violets and powders. Jack grinned when he came in. "I'm feeling much better. Charlotte's been looking after me."

Sinjen smiled, and had a look at his injury himself. The cuts were deep in some areas, but were healing well. "And how is Archie?"

"Also improved. He came down with a fever after you visited him, but it seems unrelated. You did visit him? The doctor thinks he'll be alright. Archie said he wants out of this line of work, though. I can't blame him."

Miriam knocked on the door and was let in by Charlotte. "You left me behind," she said nervously. Then she spotted Jack and froze.

"You know *him* too?" Sinjen asked. "And I thought you were such an innocent young woman."

Miriam's hand covered her chest again, then, realising that her dress was more low cut, the other one joined it. "This is the man I mentioned," she said after a moment. "I assure you, I had no idea about his real character."

"Looks like you've fallen a little way yourself," Jack told her.

"Miriam is only helping me out," Sinjen told him, hoping that they wouldn't argue. Miriam turned on her heel and said she was going home.

Jack dismissed Charlotte, and said, "I had the strangest dream about you while I was sick. I dreamt you were a vampire and you asked me to work for you."

"I am and I did. Do you want to? I need someone to keep me safe in the daytime."

"Did you tell me you'd look after my sister?" he asked.

"Yes. Is there anything else you want? I do pay my thralls; you'll be well looked after. You can leave too, whenever you wish, but I'll make you keep my true nature secret forever afterwards."

"So, it's like a normal job? For the most part."

"Yes, except that my Lady is quite likely to kill you, so it'll be dangerous. The pay will reflect that, but I think you'd have a decent chance of surviving her. You seem quick-witted, and amusing enough. That's why I want you."

"That's the only reason?"

Sinjen chuckled. "No, not the only reason."

"Then... it sounds like an adventure to me. What do I do?"

"You drink some of my blood, and say you'll serve me on the conditions we've discussed."

"And there's no catch?" Jack asked, suspiciously.

"It's all catches. You'll belong to me entirely. I won't take advantage of it, you'll just have to take my word."

"Then include that you won't take advantage of the agreement we make, and the day I die I'm released from the bond."

"That seems prudent. I agree." Sinjen put out his hand and cut into his palm with his fingernail. The wound closed in moments, but not before he was left with a palm full of blood.

Jack said, "I agree to serve you on the terms we have discussed." Then he put his lips to Sinjen's palm and swallowed his blood.

Sinjen pushed him down onto the bed and kissed him the moment he'd agreed. Jack wrapped his arms around him and began to untuck his shirt. Sinjen could feel Jack's pulse, even in his tongue, and sense the blood coursing through him, all the way through his thighs. He couldn't help but to slip his hand between Jack's legs, and feel his femoral artery through his trousers, flesh and muscle.

"We're going to have to get you some nicer clothes," he sighed, coming up for air. Jack laughed and kissed him again, letting Sinjen unbutton his shirt.

He forgot all about Miriam for the rest of the night. In fact, he forgot about everything until Harry came to get him at two in the morning.

Harry saw Jack in Sinjen's arms and rolled his eyes. "Honestly, I can't take you anywhere. Get dressed. Miriam's been more useful than you again. You have to see. Is he yours now?"

"Yes," Sinjen admitted, reaching for his shirt. "Jack, get yourself a new wardrobe, something suitable for an upper-class servant, and then go to my house. Have fun with it if you want. You aren't like the others –

you work for me, not Eliza, so just get whatever you want to wear." He handed him a wallet he'd prepared. "Make sure you arrive during the day, and tell them you're my new thrall. I'll be back home tomorrow night. Ask for the butler, and do not go upstairs until I'm there, especially at night. We have a lot of guests at the moment. Otherwise, your days are your own, but you will never harm me."

"Hmm?" Harry intoned while Jack got ready. "Make him not hurt me too, or Carlotta." Sinjen sighed, and did so.

"Where are you sleeping today?"

"I'm hardly going to tell you, am I?"

"Fine. Whatever. Come with me." Harry instructed.

Harry led Sinjen to a small and cosy reception room, designed to entertain private parties. The window was open a crack, so the air smelled fresh, even over the scent of a coal fire and forced pink and yellow hyacinth flowers. The bulbs were arranged in neat and colourful pots around the room.

Miriam was sitting with Carol and the vampire hunter. Her eyes were red, as if she'd been crying. He went straight over to her, but she shook him off.

"What on earth happened?" he asked, ignoring the others.

Miriam took a deep and shuddering breath, but sounded calm when she answered. "I went home, saw what you'd done, then I felt terrible and came back here. Only, on the way, I heard shouting and a police whistle, and I ran towards that instead. I saw your friend here on the roof, so I backed away and signalled to him. He came to me, and I told him that some vampires had been looking for him and that they cared about Miss Viola. Then we walked back here."

Harry sat down, pulling Carol onto his lap. She leant against his chest. Her eyes were misted over, so Harry must have done something to her.

"Is Viola alright?" Sinjen asked the room in general.

"Of course she is," the fledgling said, his jaw set. "You think I'd put her at risk?" Sinjen noticed he had a pronounced Russian accent. "I really cocked it up. I hired a woman who looked like my Viola, what I remember, anyway. Then he killed her, that bitter fuck."

Miriam glared at him, revolted, and he apologised, albeit insincerely, for swearing in front of a lady.

Sinjen took a deep breath and poured himself a brandy. The atmosphere in the room was extremely cold, but at least it was more like what he was used to.

"First of all," he addressed the fledgling, "what is your name?"

"I'm Alexander Varkov the fifth," he said, lifting his head and staring down the two vampires.

"Bloody hell, I had a run in with... your grandfather, maybe. Alexander something or other," Harry said, laughing. Varkov glared at him.

"Does he think Miss Viola is dead?" Miriam asked.

"I hope so," Varkov admitted.

"Alexander, I've arranged for you to join Moonlight with Harry. You should be safe there, but change your name and tell no one of your history, or you will probably die. You won't survive as a rogue, but who is this... enemy of yours?" Sinjen asked.

"That vampire is a blight. My great-grandfather had a run in with him and, ever after, he swore to end our bloodline. Naturally, we are resisting, but he's been very persistent. He killed my elder brother, tried to kill my parents and he'd kill my son too. My son doesn't know a damned thing abut what we do. I guess he'll be eight years old."

Miriam piped up, "Excuse me, but why not send your son to stay with your parents?"

"Because they rejected his mother before," Varkov said, thinking of his father's reaction back then.

"But they... they'd think you're dead? They might feel differently in that case."

Varkov looked at her, then at the floor. "I've been looking for her for ten years. I want to see her, be with her. I was a fool when I was young. I should have fought harder to stay with her and to be there for my son."

Miriam got up and went to the window. She looked out onto very little, just the back of a few houses. The scent of the pink hyacinths was slightly overwhelming, clustered as they were on the chest of drawers opposite her, with the garish yellow ones. The smell was a little nauseating, but she couldn't ignore it. She touched her chest, the pretty frills on her dress reminding her how much her situation had changed in only a few days.

Sinjen had never seemed false, whatever he was or whatever state he was in. She did believe what he had told her, even if he had lied at first. He'd been honest, for the most part. He'd said he could only waste her time and he hadn't strictly denied it when she'd asked about his inclinations. He'd asked nothing of her; he'd only wanted to know her.

She'd begun to feel like she'd stumbled into some secret world. She did like the feeling, and the new degree of comfort. Her hours were flexible enough that at this rate, she might be able to get away with working only a couple of days a week. As long as she still made her rent money, she shouldn't be left in such a bad place. Sinjen had already given her enough that, if she was careful, she might live for a year or two just on his generosity. An advantage of having so few needs on her own. Yet, they had made no real agreement between them, as he had with Jack.

Victor Bickerstaff

Chapter 12

Sinjen nodded at Harry, who waved his hand and compelled Carol to sleep. He would make her forget everything else later. "Miriam may be right, Alexander. Your family would be the best place to send your son, wouldn't it?"

Varkov frowned and looked at his feet. "I do know that. I want to see her, though. I won't be able to when they go to my home, and I have no guarantee that Viola would be treated properly. I don't think she'd be the sort of woman to give her child over to other people either."

"Well, I could take her there during the day and explain the situation. I assume that you wouldn't want them to know that you'd become a..." Miriam began.

Varkov laughed. "Hell, no, they'd kill me. I mean, heck no. They'd consider it a stain on the family honour. It would never be allowed, and it has never been allowed in the past."

"Oh, it's happened before?" Harry grinned. "To whom?"

Varkov rolled his eyes. "It happens every so often. Some vampires think it's funny to turn us, I suppose. From what I've heard, it's almost impossible for a turned vampire hunter to survive. At least, ever since St. Daminh."

"You know about him?" Sinjen asked, surprised.

"Of course. All vampire hunters know about him. He worked with a few of us, including my family, slipped us a lot of useful information to clear a path for him. He paid spectacularly, founded a couple of sects, too. Though the first was wiped out."

Sinjen raised an eyebrow. "How amazing, I had no idea."

Harry frowned. "He was a monster, he wiped out my old clan. Southern Cross was wonderful. We were so close, and so few of us survived."

"My word," Varkov sighed, his voice almost desirous, "you couldn't be Harry Balcom? The insane, drug-peddling killer of fair young ladies? Do you have *any* idea how much your head or heart is worth?"

Sinjen laughed. Harry shot him an irritated glance, and Miriam looked between them both, stunned. "Excuse me, Mr. Varkov, but have you ever heard of a vampire called Sinjen Carlyle?"

Sinjen glanced at her affectionately.

"No. Is that him? He can't be of any particular note, I suppose. If I don't know him, then he's never been mentioned on our bounties."

"Maybe I don't leave survivors?" Sinjen grinned.

"Shut up, Sinjen. You're a pussycat," Harry said. "And you – you're one of us now. You'll have to consider a new line of work."

"Did one of you bite me?" Varkov asked.

"No," Sinjen said, before anyone else could answer. "Our dearest Miriam here informed me that there was a stray fledgling running around. We just happened to be in town. You know, Whitby is popular at the moment because of Bram Stoker. A lot of us like to stop by. You weren't subtle."

Miriam turned back to the window, unsure why Sinjen had lied. She'd trust him for now and ask him later.

"So, you're courting a human. Do you intend to turn her?" Varkov asked.

Miriam looked back at them, horrorstruck.

"No. I just like her. She won't come to harm, but you should avoid associating with me until you're fully settled in Moonlight." He took off his jacket and rolled up his sleeve to show Varkov. "Do you know what this is?"

"It can't be," Varkov gasped. "Daylight is gone. Is that real?" He looked at Harry, who nodded.

"Two of us yet live. I'd like to advise you before you go to Italy, and you shouldn't wait too long before leaving. The first thing is that you'll have to feed again, once or twice, if you want to maintain your health. May we speak alone?"

"I'll look after the fledgling, Sinjen," Harry said.

"You will, but think about it. It's better if I give him some advice, given his difficult circumstances, yes? Miss Miriam can sort out your family. If your boy is taken to your family home, Miss Viola can aim to go there a week or so later. But, you'll need a place to sleep, won't you? I can help you lie low for a little while. Harry will help you to integrate."

"You both seem very helpful," Varkov said, looking between them. "What's in it for you?"

"That's a great question. The answer, for me, is that I'd like to know about this rogue. Call it a small revival of my past interests. Harry tells me that he's well-known, and I'm under orders from my mistress to build my reputation, through scandal, preferably."

"And who is your mistress?" Varkov asked. Sinjen told him, and he turned to Harry, who nodded. "No, that can't be. Is she nearby?"

"She's gone to Germany," Sinjen explained. "I'd strongly suggest that you leave before she gets back. Get yourself a proper grave, too, because if you wish to travel by sea then you'll want the soil. Harry will help you with that, I don't doubt. For now, take a walk with me, sir. Henry will escort my dear lady to the street where she lives."

"Will I now?" Harry said coldly.

"You will, after she has found Miss Viola. Harry, wake Carol first, and I'll explain anything else on the way home."

Harry regarded him, and then Miriam, for a few moments, before stretching and agreeing, "Alright, Sinjen. I'll take care of the women and children, but this had better be worth it."

"Of course it will, my dear. You'll have a powerful new recruit for Moonlight, and I'll have a little glory. That's fair, isn't it?"

Miriam leant against the window, unsure of what to think. Sinjen kissed her on the cheek and tapped her pocket, where she still held the key to his sleeping place.

Varkov and Sinjen took a walk together, this time along the beach. A bobby cautioned them to take care after the murders, but Sinjen only waved his hand and sent the man elsewhere. Varkov watched with an unexpected degree of curiosity.

Sinjen began, "You seem to be adjusting well. I suppose you must have wondered what would happen if you turned, before now?"

"A little bit. I guess it's easier, since I already know what's happened to me." Varkov admitted, "I had strong feelings about turning once, but now I don't. I only want that rogue dead. He's been a bane to us, a blight on my family. As long as he dies, I think I can move on."

"Do you need to kill him yourself?"

"I'd like to. You don't want me to, do you? You want to do it. You think I should consider my future, is that it?"

"Yes," Sinjen grinned. "Leave him to me, and keep yourself out of trouble. Do you know his name – is it his real one?"

"He goes by Victor Bickerstaff. He has for as long as I've ever known. You understand what I mean; they usually have aliases. I don't know if I have the entire story. They say that my great-grandfather failed to kill him, and he's been out for revenge ever since. It's true that each subsequent generation has had to deal with him. He must be near three hundred judging by his strength, but we've never been able to learn more about him and we've done everything we can. He was the one who tried to kill me when I was young, the one who scarred my face and neck.

"Sometimes he comes for us, other times he can be gone for decades without even a whisper. He's killed more of my blood than any other vampire. The problem is, he doesn't generally leave again until he's killed one of us, or been defeated."

"But that's good news," Sinjen pointed out. "You died. If he knew that, would he leave for a while?"

"Perhaps," Alexander admitted.

106

"Then let's tell him. Let me take care of Bickerstaff. I admit, I don't know his real name, but that one can't be right. Harry seems to know him, though. Would you recognise him if you saw him?"

"Would I know him?" Alexander asked. "I'd know. My whole family would."

"Very well." Sinjen sighed. "Now, about your wife. There are a few things you should know, if you wish to spend time with her without killing her. That includes that you must be fully fed first, or your desire will be confused. Also, be aware, it's not impossible for the two of you to conceive. Your fertility will drastically decrease in time. But for now, at least, you are as close to life as you will be, ever after.

"I'll set you up for a few days. I have a place you can rest, and thralls who will protect you during the day. I'm the only one who knows about it – a little townhouse. Miriam can send your wife there, and after a week or so you should leave with Harry, work hard and adjust to your new life."

"Do you know who turned me?" Varkov asked.

"I told you. I have no idea. About a third of the British vampires I know are in the North currently, and any of them might have come to visit. Why do you ask?"

"My dagger is missing. I guess that's to be expected. The sentimental value, though. I know I couldn't use it anymore."

"I'm sorry." Sinjen took out his cheque book and wrote something out for Varkov. "This is nothing like the value of a vampire slayer's weapon, but it may help you to get established. Now, Moonlight is generous with its recruits, as Lord Blackthorn likes to keep his clan in his pocket. If you are smart, you will take this money, his too, and hide it for a while, until you can replace what he will give you. He is generous and you will live well, but you'll be at his mercy unless you are independent. He penalises that, though, so plan well. Under no circumstances let Harry anywhere near your finances. And give yourself a new name and backstory. Don't be amazed when you meet famous vampires, or reveal your knowledge of them, it'll raise suspicions. I hope, besides Bickerstaff, no one will recognise you by sight. If he's really a rogue, as Harry indicated, then you would be unlikely to see him anyway."

"I barely recognise myself." Varkov sighed. "I was so disfigured. It's strange to see my face as it would have been. Bickerstaff has nothing to do with Moonlight?"

"I don't believe so. If I wanted to, do you have any idea how I might lure him out?"

"Not really, though he does like to watch fights. It's something he has in common with some of my own family, and from time to time he's been seen at one, especially if there's a well-known fighter there. I can't offer you anything at present, but if you kill him, I'll owe you a favour."

Sinjen smiled. "You need to survive, and be accepted, before your favour is worth anything. However, if I can kill him I will."

Wolfsbane

Chapter 13

Miriam knocked on Viola's door at eight in the morning, aware that the woman would most likely be exhausted. Viola opened the door looking quite cheerful, although her hair was already escaping its bun. Outside of work she looked rather pleasant and proper; it seemed she was leading something of a double life. Miriam wondered if she was too.

Miriam was also back in her usual clothing. "Miss Viola, may we speak? Mr. Varkov sent me. The one who has been looking for you," she said, with a glance through the door.

She could see their son getting ready for school, tucking his slate and pencil into his satchel, then searching around for his necktie. She smiled, a little affectionately, over Viola's shoulder before turning back to the woman, who looked concerned, let her in, and shut the door behind her.

"What does he want?" she asked.

"Do you know what his family did?" Miriam asked.

"He told me once, but you wouldn't believe me if I told you."

"If I told you that he'd been killed, and was now changed, would you understand me?"

Viola's eyes widened. "You mean he was defeated? He was always so strong. What now? His family can't find out."

Miriam exhaled with relief. At least she knew and her loyalty was with him, and not his family. That would make things easier. "Alexander is hoping that you might go to stay with him, at least for a little while. He's also requested that I take your son to his family home for his protection. I may be able to do this with or without you, whichever would be easier. The hope is that you might both be accepted, in light of his passing. What is the boy's name?"

"He's called Alexander," Viola said, wiping her eyes. "If it's okay, I'd like to send my boy to school, then I'll come with you to the guest house. I told my son his father was dead. He doesn't know anything that might affect him, not for now. Does he really want to see me? Even still?"

Miriam nodded and promised to come back in an hour. Sinjen had given her enough that she could afford a carriage halfway across the country, if needed.

She wandered down to the beach and had a few jellied eels while she waited, listening to the waves and watching the beachgoers. They were timid of the sea and the cold, but amused enough to look for shells and jet, or else visit the stands and attractions by the pier.

She'd bought a new stole and was glad of it, feeling the cold north wind blow across the town.

The coach pulled up to the guest house. It was a little larger than she expected, built of dull grey stone with its own grounds. The plants were a bit stunted, gnarled and hardened by the unforgiving sea air, but a jagged row of sea buckthorn protected the rest of the planting from the worst of the damage. The bright orange berries were dramatic this time of year. They stood out on their dark stems against the white of the sky and sea. Miriam had noticed many times the way that England was prone to desaturate in the winter months. The landscape became almost grayscale between the bare black trees, white sky and misty low clouds.

"This is where you grew up?" she asked Viola. The proximity to the cliffs made her a little unsettled.

"It's nice, isn't it? In summer, even spring, I assure you, the gardens are very cheerful. We have so many bulbs, but for now, it's all resting. The weather steals the show here. When there's a storm, those grey stone walls feel like a fortress, unshakable and warm. I hope my parents are still alive, but... then again..." Her eyes filled, and Miriam put her hand on hers.

"What should we do? Do you want me to go in first and look around, or should we just brave it?"

Viola sighed. "Let's go in. I don't want to play around. They'll have me or they won't. They were cold before and cast me out. The way I approach this won't matter."

Miriam studied her with compassion. She'd become so hardened, but she had her reasons.

"Let me check first, I want to see who's in. I think we should go straight for... Alexander the fourth, is that his name?"

Viola laughed. "Yes. There's a certain convenience to such a predictable naming system, isn't there?"

Miriam went inside and found an older man sitting alone in the reception room. He was hunched over in his chair, reading a newspaper, but stood when she entered.

"Good afternoon, Miss," he said, hurrying to make himself appear more accommodating. "But, I must apologise, we have no vacancies at present. We are partnered with another guest house – I could give you their address."

She shook her head. "I'm hoping to meet someone named Alexander Varkov. Might he be here?"

The man escorted her upstairs, not questioning further. He left her for a moment in a small waiting area and bustled away to find the occupant of this floor. The room was cheerful enough, with a bowl of bold narcissus flowers brightening the windowsills. She looked around at the curious mementos on the wall. Rubbings of tombstones from the looks of things, as well as stakes. On a few plinths were skulls with long canines, most with bricks wedged between the skull and lower jaw. It was rather odd.

She stood to look at a few more keepsakes. There were a number of jewellery items and silver objects, including pendants with twisted or braided hair inside them. A few strange rings were displayed, too, set with what might be carved teeth as gems. She jumped when the man returned and told her she could enter.

Alexander the fourth was sitting at his desk. He was imposing and severe-looking, but had been disfigured by scars, visible even where they cut gaps in his neat beard. He wore a coat with a thick fur collar, and was missing a considerable chunk of his right index finger. He waved her towards a seat, and she tried not to look too frightened as she sat down.

"I'm afraid I have bad news about your son," she began, nervously. He didn't give a reaction but watched her, his expression like a wolf watching his prey. After a pause she continued, "He's dead. He died looking for his son. I found him, and his mother. It was the... it was his wish that they would return here and find safety with you. He was not able to..."

"Obviously, he did not defeat Bickerstaff if he is dead, girl. Why are you involved in all this?"

She faltered for a moment, "I-I'm a friend of Miss Viola. She's waiting outside. Should I send for her?"

"It's just the boy I'm interested in," he said.

Miriam's temper flared. "Well, you don't get to split apart his family, when you abandoned them both once. Your son didn't want that. He wanted them both protected."

Alexander laughed. "Alright, and what do you propose will happen to the boy and the little strumpet?"

She frowned. "I'd suggest you start by treating Viola with respect. She's worked hard to raise the boy, who looks, if you'll forgive me, very like your own son. They did want to marry, as I understand the situation. We... we can't change anything now, but unless you have any other sons, this is the family you have left. You could have worse."

He leant back. "I'll take them both. Did you tell her father who you came here with? The man you just saw. Her mother has passed."

"No. I didn't know who to look for. Your son was very concerned that she might not be accepted back here. Would her father... object?"

He smiled slightly. "No. He missed his daughter very much. I myself... regretted my..."

She looked at him with a little more compassion. "Rash decision?"

"My son had been betrothed, since he was still in his cradle, to a young lady from another family... like ours. I did not foresee that he would be so angry with me, that he would make himself unappealing to her. I should have made a different decision, in hindsight. Will that suffice? I don't wish to see her at present, but for my son's sake I'll take care of them both. His mother will be... less grieved, I think. To find that our lineage is not over. Not just yet, anyway."

Miriam nodded. "I believe Viola has a few loose ends to take care of before she will return here. You can expect her in a week or two, but she wishes her son to return immediately. Do I have your assurance that both will be truly welcome?"

He took her hand between both of his. "They will both be cared for. Let her know, though, that the boy's life will be as hard as our own. He may well die young, like my brothers and uncles. As long as Bickerstaff lives, particularly, I can't guarantee him anything."

"I think the idea is that he survives the next few months or years, at least. Are you and your wife the only two... vampire hunters here?"

"No. There are six of us. We have never been attacked directly, and we have more protection here than you might expect."

"May I ask you something?" Miriam hazarded. He nodded. "Do... do you think there are any vampires who deserve to live?"

He blinked at her as if she had asked something foolish. "They don't live. They are dead and their existence can only cause death. They may be, or seem, charming, but there is nothing there. They are possessed corpses; their souls must be put to rest. None can live without taking lives. Why do you ask this?"

She shook her head. "Only a fancy. I read too many books, perhaps."

He smiled sympathetically. "If you had met one, there would be no fancy. They are enticing, but it's all a lie. Their facade of humanity is only a mask for the evil that they truly are. They can no longer appreciate death, humanity, or what they lost when they... turned. They are an abomination."

She nodded, curtsied politely and retreated to the carriage.

She got inside and wrapped her stole around her. Viola peered at her curiously, but she only assured the woman that everything was alright. She promised that she would explain the rest soon, but for now could only look out of the window at the sheets of grey cloud in the distance, and at the mist over the gorse and heather of the moors.

The Burial Chamber

Chapter 14

Viola had decided her son would be brought to his grandfather's house before dark. Viola left, just after her son, to go to the house where Varkov would meet her when he woke. A place Sinjen had arranged.

Miriam didn't book her own transport. The cottage Sinjen had given her the key to was near enough, and she could walk a few miles, especially when she was in a mood like this. She almost didn't look where she was going, even when a flurry of snow fell, pelting her hair and attire. She pressed her hands into her pockets. Even in her new gloves and fur she wouldn't rely on him. She'd had her faith before, even if she'd never been devout. When Sinjen had called himself her meal ticket, she'd really been hurt by the insinuation.

She was half-soaked before she arrived at the pretty thatched cottage, and unpleasantly cold. Water dripped from her neck and down her décolletage. Her layers had protected her from the worst of it, but she probably looked half-drowned, her curls and braids flattened by the weather. Her hair had been styled, but only tended towards a mild curl without effort. She wouldn't bother doing that again for a few days.

She knocked, hoping it was the right place, and was let in by a serious-looking but attractive man. Older than her, but without many signs of age.

"I'm here to see Sinjen Carlyle. He sent for me..." she began.

His servant smiled at her, brought her a hand towel, and took her coat, hat and stole to dry them. The house was warm to the point of being almost stuffy, but this was very welcome. "It would be my pleasure to show you to him. He's asleep in a coffin, below. Should I come with you?"

"What do I call you?" she asked gently, following him through a small door, but when the man answered her, she wasn't concentrating enough to remember. "This basement," she breathed, as Sinjen's thrall led her down stone steps. "What is this?"

The servant laughed. "A copy of a copy of, perhaps, a legend. It's supposed to be a tomb, the one our Lord Jesus was buried in, at least according to the replica in Ripon Cathedral."

"Is-is that right?" she asked.

The servant frowned and looked back at her. "Maybe, or maybe not. If it was the one, my guess is that he could not rest here. I think he only built it as a joke, or maybe to check. He never usually sleeps here; this is just a game to him. Take my candle, and it might be sensible to pray, but do not be scared. He would not have sent for you if he meant to kill you."

"Have you worked for him long?"

"Oh, yes. He's been good to us all, but if you wish him dead then take this, here." He handed her a knife longer than her forearm. It was unusual: bronze, plain and carved. She gazed at it, afraid for a moment to pick it up, but she did, then looked closer. No Star of David, but crosses, fish, menorah, some other things – a pentacle? Other symbols she could not recognise. She shook her head. She couldn't tell which signs were right, to think about it was confusing. Had this belonged to the vampire hunter?

She turned it over in her hand, feeling very strange, and walked down the stairs. The path was dark and narrow, but the walls were white, as were the uneven stairs leading into a small square room. The servant left through another tunnel, which led away and likely came up in the garden. The whole room was whitewashed, except for a few bare stones. In a small indent were some candles, enough to light the room, as compact as it was.

It was comfortable here, underground. She wouldn't choose it as a home, but beneath the earth, and a house like this, perhaps a whole family could be pleasantly warm all year even without a fire.

Just before her, on a raised stone slab, she could see a coffin, large and finely made. For a moment she felt quite dizzy, and took the time to unfasten, brush and braid her hair before she made any further decisions.

When she was presentable, she knelt before it, touching the woodwork. She shut her eyes and pressed her head against the grain.

Time passed. She would have doubted that she had fallen asleep at all, except that her knees and hips ached. The servant from before had woken her, replacing some of the most melted candles. She hadn't meant to doze off, but she had been travelling and it had been so cold today.

He put the dirk back into her hands and assured her that she was safe. Miriam looked at him groggily. "Is he *truly* good to you?"

The man smiled. "I am nothing, I never was. I was alone with no family. Sinjen saved me from a workhouse, like a lot of us. He's given us a better life and he's asked so little of me. Kill him, though, and I'll be free. He hasn't left me to anyone, but I don't know what I'd do afterwards. My only real duty is to protect him, but not from you. I'm too old now, I suppose, to become a vampire hunter, but maybe I would have. Some of his friends are evil. His mistress is... She's horrific beyond reason, but sometimes I wonder what it would take to kill one. It would feel like killing anyone else, surely, and I don't think I have the stomach for that."

She was left alone again, contemplating the day and her choices. Alexander the fourth had seemed like he would keep his word, and though he had been intimidating, he'd had something warm about him. He would have been able to kill Sinjen in a heartbeat.

She'd been hesitating, she knew that. There wouldn't be too much daylight left, but this trust exercise was very strange. She was afraid to open the coffin. Anything might be inside it, or it could be empty. Did he want her to kill him, or was this just so that the servant would report back?

She took a deep breath and lifted the lid, keeping her eyes closed as she did. He was there when she opened them. She knew he was dead at once – his body was vacant, like a shell, but unchanged. So, he really was prepared to let her kill him if she wanted to? She sighed. Perhaps he just didn't want to wonder about it.

She leant closer and examined him. He wasn't breathing, and his expression was almost peaceful, his hands resting on his chest. Miriam reached out and touched one of his hands. It was cold and slid to his side.

She picked it up and pressed the edge of the knife against his palm. It left a nasty burn, which remained on his skin.

Miriam put the knife on the floor, her hands shaking, and paced around the room for a little while. She returned, unable to resist taking another look at him.

He had a few gold rings on, fairly plain. Did he always sleep in a full suit? She supposed he wouldn't crumple it, really; it wasn't like it would move, or be softened by the heat of his body. He wouldn't sweat. Perhaps it made no difference.

Miriam touched the fabric of his suit, a very fine wool blend, if she had to guess. Surprisingly plain, but beautifully made and fitted. In the pocket of his jacket, she could see a gold cigarette case. She was a little afraid to touch it, but in the end did. She lit one and replaced his items before going upstairs.

The servant considered her with a raised eyebrow. "You don't look like the sort of lady who would smoke," he said with mild amusement. She noticed that he was younger than she'd first guessed, maybe around thirty-two.

"May I smoke in the garden?" she asked. He chuckled and opened the back door for her, then brought out her stole, which was now dry. It was a very practical space, with neat vegetable beds and a chicken coop in the back. A straight garden path cut down the middle and there were trained fruit trees along the brick walls, all covered with a light layer of snow. "Do you live here? All the time?"

The man nodded. "It's pretty, isn't it? He pays us very fairly and he's so rarely home that the place might as well be mine. He only asks that I keep the pantry well stocked and the master bedroom and basement ready for him. He's really rather unfussy. If he comes to stay alone then it's usually just to read for a little while, or to take a few of my apples back with him. Most often, it's to stash a drunk friend or two in the basement."

Miriam giggled, then looked at her cigarette. Her fingers were tingling and she felt a little light-headed. The servant laughed. "Was that one of his? I'm sorry, it's anyone's guess what could be in that. You should be alright; I've done the same before."

"I can see now that I've been a little unwise," she said, and offered it to him to smoke, which he did. "I'm very sorry, but I've forgotten your name."

"Richard Wright," he said with a smile.

When Sinjen emerged from his sleep he didn't have to wonder if Miriam had been to see him. The knife was on the floor by his coffin and he could hear laughter. He found Miriam and Richard in the garden, feeding the chickens. Richard was showing her his Old English Game birds, which he kept for eggs and cockfights. Sinjen occasionally brought a few to his parties for the vampires, who got excited about all that. They were a difficult breed. Even the hens tended to fight one another, but Richard always kept them well and in good shape.

He'd wondered about the morality of cockfighting from time to time, but after he'd met Richard's birds, he had to admit that some of them were psychotic enough that they probably lived for the challenge. The practice had long been illegal, but could still be found if you knew where to look.

He watched for a little while as Miriam ran around to avoid a particularly burly rooster which had managed to escape. His servant wrangled it back into the pen, likely sustaining minor injuries.

"Are you both having fun?" he asked after a minute or two. They both started laughing and Miriam apologised for pinching one of his cigarettes. He grinned – that explained it. "What would you like to do tonight, Miriam? You can stay here if you like, you must have had a busy day. Is the boy safe?"

She nodded, and explained everything that had happened. "Then, stay and rest, enjoy your day off. I have no doubt Mr. Wright will escort you home safely. I'm going to spend the night looking for this rogue and taking care of Varkov. I don't know exactly what to expect."

"But, I couldn't," Miriam began, "it would be a bit..."

Sinjen laughed. "I assume you just spent the day considering killing me, after visiting a vampire hunter's house and arranging for the adoption of a bastard child. You'll be alright to help Richard bake one of his apple pies and relax for an evening. You'll take good care of her, won't you, Richard?"

"Of course, sir."

"Well, good. I'll leave a few more cigarettes on the mantelpiece then. Richard, tomorrow, please would you bring that dagger to my main residence and spend some time training my new thrall."

Richard bowed, and Sinjen made his way back to Jack, though he stopped on the way to feed on a night watchman.

Jack was happy enough. Sinjen showed him around and introduced him to Carlotta and her ladies, as well as Harry and Lord Marlais.

He was pleased to see that Jack had the right temperament for the house. It wasn't considered polite for a vampire to feed on the personal thrall of another, but it would still be better for him if he made friends.

"So, what are my duties?" Jack asked, when Sinjen showed him into his room.

"Just, you know... help me with tasks, make sure things are working well enough at home and guard me when I sleep. Don't look at me when I'm sleeping, though, I hate that. Just check the room, lock the doors and stay nearby while I rest. I'll have to hypnotise you so that you're immune to the suggestions of other vampires, but that's easy enough. Oh, and come and meet Lady Skinner. You don't need to use her title, she's only a knight. A very impressive figure, though, try not to be too amazed." Seeing Jack's expression, he laughed. "I am really happy that you accepted my offer."

"I think I am too," Jack said, and took him in his arms. "But maybe I can meet them a bit later."

Sinjen kissed him. "Oh, alright then."

Jack grinned. "You're rather accommodating, aren't you?"

Sinjen shrugged, and kissed him again. "I'm happy, and yes. You'll find out soon enough what kind of a disaster I am. Oh, would you be a dear and order about a hundred towels and blankets to be shipped to this address tomorrow? Then phone all the people on that list on my desk and ask for the usual. Then you just want to call the last name and ask for a medium-sized bonfire, a few log burners and tents, and absolute litres of water to be boiled. Alright?" He handed Jack the sheet of paper, realising there were several very similar.

Jack's eyes widened. "Alright. What's it for?"

"A pool party. You can come, it's fine. Stick with Sora and avoid Lord Marlais, to be safe. He's a bit of a bastard at my events. Oh, and wear something warm. It's such a relief though, I won't need guests. You see those weapons on the wall? Two things: choose one, and learn how to use it, alright? You don't want to be unarmed here."

"Okay," Jack said, looking mildly alarmed. His eyes scanned the collection of weaponry displayed in Sinjen's room. "Can I have the whip?"

Sinjen laughed. "Yes, I can teach you that one. Don't ask, though. I don't want to explain why I know that particular skill."

Jack sighed, and pushed Sinjen towards the bed. "I won't ask. Just take your shirt off before I do it for you."

A Fight with a Friend

Chapter 15

Harry came to town with him again. He was in a bit of a funny mood, because he hadn't had much luck with Carlotta. He wouldn't talk about it, though, so he'd probably said something stupid to her.

"So, who's this rogue?" Sinjen asked.

Harry glared at him.

"You know him, but I asked around and nobody knows who he is. So it's a false name."

Harry sighed. "I told you that I'm not helping and you should just leave it alone."

"I don't want to. I'm curious to meet him. Who goes out of his way to antagonise vampire hunters?"

"He has his reasons, but he's very dangerous. He's got a considerable bounty, no clan, and it's been that way for years. You don't need me to tell you how rare that is. Yes, he's using a false name. He's not famous any more, but he once was."

"Other people would know him?" Sinjen asked, watching Harry's brow furrow.

"No, probably not, but they would know his name."

"How can I find him?"

Harry laughed. "He'll have been watching you for days, I bet. He'll find you if he wants to, but you won't be able to find him. It's a good job you moved that boy during the day. Where is your fledgling?"

"He's not my fledgling is he?" Sinjen sighed. "But, he'll be with his wife."

Harry stayed quiet and watched the road. After a while, Sinjen asked him how it was going with Carlotta. "Bloody badly, isn't it? She's just keeping her distance; I can't make any kind of progress."

"You won't make any progress if you don't seem reliable. I'm her type, not you."

Harry turned to him with a scowl.

"That's advice. She likes men who are dependable and put together. Hard workers, good providers, moral—"

"You're the single most immoral person I know," Harry objected. "There's barely anything you won't stoop to, just for fun, and probably nothing if it would keep you alive. You're a laughing stock, a simpering fool, a weakling, a spineless—"

"Stop the car, Harry," Sinjen said coldly, his face a frozen mask.

"You know what, I bloody will," Harry said and drew the car to a halt in front of the wooden gate of a fallow field.

126

Sinjen got out and neatened his clothes. He removed his gloves and put them in his pocket, then took off his hat and jacket, and left them over the car door. Harry did the same. They walked to the field.

"Sinjen, you're a dog. Someone ought to remind you."

"It would be nice, someday, if people could let me forget. Why have you taken against me all of a sudden?" he asked, looking no less cold.

"Because you're a nosy, overly ambitious whore and I'm tired of it."

"Oh, you mean because Carlotta is still holding a candle for me instead of a waste of space like you?" He grinned, seeing Harry's fury, and stepped aside to dodge a wild blow. He efficiently tripped Harry up as he did and the man fell forward. Before he could get up, Sinjen kicked him hard in the ribs and heard several bones break. This didn't faze Harry as much as he'd hoped. Harry threw a handful of dirt in his face, then careened into him, knocking the air from his lungs and toppling them both. They punched and slashed at one another on the ground, until their shirts were sliced to ribbons and both were bloody, then Sinjen caught Harry in his injured ribs with his knee. Harry cried out and Sinjen was able to pin him down, placing his fingernails against his throat, ready to sever his spine. Harry shouted, but gave up the fight.

He sighed. "Alright. Maybe I haven't been *entirely* fair."

Sinjen patted him on the shoulder and let him get up. "I won't hold this against you, then."

"You mean you won't feed me to Eliza? That's sweet," Harry said, a little bitterly. "Actually, you're a lot stronger than I'd expected. I'd heard you weren't up to much."

"I don't want them giving me dangerous work, do I? I have enough to deal with as it is."

They went back to the car. Harry had some whiskey from a flask in his glovebox. He passed it to Sinjen while they waited for their injuries to heal. "We can go to my place and get a clean shirt," Sinjen suggested. "Miriam might still be there."

Harry turned to him and asked, "Do you like her or not? I can't tell with you."

"I like her well enough," he said, fishing a cigarette out of his case.

Miriam had already gone home. Sinjen asked Richard if he knew of any boxing matches, or similar, that were on at present.

"None that I know of until next weekend, sir," he said, taking in their ripped-up shirts and muddy clothing. Harry was already half-naked before he'd come in with the washbasin. His figure was so impressive that he wondered how these vampires could avoid being permanently distracted by each other's looks.

Sinjen also undressed and started to wash the blood off his skin. He was leaner than Harry, rather sculpted and pretty, but his mood was poor and Richard didn't enjoy that any more than anyone else. He tended to become harsh and irritable. When he was like that, even his hands were scarier, his mannerisms became sharper and more deliberate, and his eyes even more unfeeling.

"Alright, let's go," Sinjen directed, the second he was done. Even Harry didn't bother objecting, it wasn't worth it when Sinjen was in a dangerous mood.

Sinjen left when they arrived in Whitby, and Harry let him, feeling as though he'd taken a few steps back with his relationships. Sinjen took a path along the seafront, trying to calm down before he found Miriam.

He spirited into her room when he got near enough, but found her asleep. Her room was still rather unremarkable, so he left again and brought her back an oil painting of a ship braving a turbulent sea. He hung it above her fireplace. Hopefully she'd like it.

Sinjen decided to take a walk over the rooftops of the main shopping street, in case anyone he knew was around. He stopped on an empty terrace and had a smoke, thinking about what had happened so far.

A man tapped his shoulder after a little while. The rogue had turned up. He hadn't made a sound.

Sinjen offered him a cigarette. "Bickerstaff?"

"That's right."

"I've been taking an interest in your goings-on. What on earth are you doing antagonising vampire hunters?"

Bickerstaff laughed. "They started it, I'm afraid. They wouldn't give me a moment's peace."

"So you've created a character? Why do they think you're doing what you are doing?"

"I couldn't tell you for certain, but I've fed them a little tale over the years," he said, without smiling.

Sinjen scanned him critically and the man backed away a little. He was in black again; his hair was unnaturally dark against his fair skin. He had a beard and moustache, not kept well. His whiskers were straggly and thin on the sides; it was a very distracting feature. Sinjen touched his shoulder to confirm his suspicions. "Your clothing is padded – are you wearing a costume?"

Bickerstaff laughed. "I have to change my appearance from time to time, I gather I have a bounty. More than one, actually, human and vampire."

"You aren't sure? You're so out of the loop of vampire society that you haven't seen it? I could check for you."

The man shook his head. "If I gave you my real name, then word might get out that I'm still alive. I'm not meant to be. What are you? Moonlight?" Sinjen rolled up his sleeve and showed the man the golden brand on his arm. "That can't be," the man said, sounding amazed but not afraid. "Daylight was wiped out."

"There are two of us still kicking. Prisoners of a sort, with Nightfall," Sinjen said, turning away and looking down at the town.

It was late enough that almost no one was still walking around; those who were were either drunk, poor or especially cautious. He chuckled, watching a young man climb out of one window and in through another. "What do you think? A thief or an affair?"

"He's bedding his employer's wife, he does it most nights," Bickerstaff explained. "I was a little curious myself."

"So that's your plan? You're just going to keep running until someone kills you? Or what? Start an illegal clan?"

"Oh no, that would bring a lot of heat. But I don't know what more I can do. I really messed up at the beginning. I didn't know any better at the time, but I was branded a criminal. There is no one who could speak for me. You aren't here for my bounty, are you?"

Sinjen frowned. "I have some sympathy, but I can't speak for you. Nobody would trust my word, but I'll think about some options. And no, I'm just watching. I'm concerned about the fledgling."

"He's already dead," Bickerstaff said. "There's nothing that can be done for him."

"What do you mean?"

"His family will get rid of him. They won't stop until he's at rest. They won't find the body and then they'll know what has happened. In all likelihood, they'll find him soon, and he'll know that. Has he fled?"

Sinjen shook his head.

"Then he's not trying to fight it. If he cared, he'd be gone. I have to go."

Bickerstaff vanished. Sinjen looked around and saw Harry watching them from the opposite roof. He spirited to the terrace, the place Bickerstaff had just vacated.

"So you had a bit of luck then," Harry said. He still looked unhappy.

"I suppose so."

"It would be better if we left. I don't want to be here when the hunters turn up. I'm worth a fair amount to them, as Alexander pointed out."

"I'll probably just stick around and watch."

Harry turned to him with concern. "Look, I'm sorry for what I said. I didn't mean those things, really. Have I... upset you?"

Sinjen sighed. "If it was that easy to make me kill myself, I'd be dead. Don't worry about it, I hear worse all the time."

"I'll stay with you then, for this. We'll have better odds if there's trouble."

Sinjen raised an eyebrow. "You actually care?"

Harry clapped him on the shoulder. "What's your next move?"

"I'll go back to Miriam and ask her to go and see the vampire hunters. I want the story. Unless you will just tell me how you know Bickerstaff?"

"I will not, but tell me what they say, I'd be curious to hear their version."

"She'd be the best person to go, I expect. I'll have her speak to Viola too, about little Alexander's safety. His father should probably leave. I can't imagine there would be any risk to him at Moonlight."

"Sure, but hunters like this would wait for him to come out again. They might only be in England now because they're watching a target. Might have been waiting for generations. Or did they arrive recently?" Harry asked.

"No, Viola said they've been here for at least ten years, but that might be interesting to know."

Storm by the Sea

Chapter 16

Miriam pulled up in the carriage, as Sinjen had directed. He had woken her with kisses in the small hours. She was a little ashamed to admit that she hadn't even been afraid. She'd pulled her blankets up over her chest and he'd taken the faded, second-hand sheets in his hands and promised to replace them. Where did he think she lived, anyway? Her little apartment wasn't nice enough to justify his spending. She'd sighed and let him speak, before he returned home.

Viola had been informed of the danger to Alexander, but the news only caused her suffering. Miriam could tell, even if she tried to hide it. The fledgling vampire was sleeping when she came to see her.

More disturbingly still, the papers had reported that a woman's body had washed up on the beach that morning. The written description matched Viola. Perhaps it had been a coincidence, or perhaps the rogue was still searching for her, but she didn't like it. There was too much excitement in Whitby at present. Even if Sinjen had assured her that the vampire tourists were very well-behaved, it was an unsettling thought that, as a night owl, she might have passed a few and not even known.

When she pulled up to the grey house, it was drastically different than before. There was a cold sun today and the garden's anemones stood out in the bright sunlight, as did the delicate purple monkshood, its leaves slightly mottled in spite of the healthy flowers. The rest of the garden remained quite dormant. She could see now that the building was stained darkly, worn and discoloured by the tempestuous sea weather.

In summer though, Viola was right, these gardens would be vibrant and cheerful. They, even in this season, were neatly arranged and obviously cared for. Perhaps not so much as Mr. Wright's little garden.

Again, she requested to see Mr. Varkov, and again it was allowed without question. He took longer to appear this time. It was early in the morning, so she examined the waiting room with more careful attention than before. The room had tall windows and heavy mud-green curtains. It appeared that this family rented the entire top floor, so they had the full benefit of the view over the cliffs and weatherbeaten landscape beyond their own protected land. She could see dark, windswept clouds, weeping with rain over the sea. They'd make it over here and hit Whitby too, she expected. She might throw a few extra coals on the fire tonight, and be grateful for Sinjen's generosity, if there was going to be a storm.

She jumped as Alexander the fourth called her, and consciously made an effort to appear less hurried and nervous as he directed her towards his desk. He seemed so relaxed, yet somehow that made her more frightened. His fur collar was so pretty, contrasting with the scars over his face and neck, dozens, a little raised and much clearer in the sunlight.

"I, um..." she began and then faltered.

"Do you wish to report a problematic undead?" he asked.

"It's not... precisely that. Whitby has had two deaths, of women resembling Miss Viola, and... I'd like to ask about Victor Bickerstaff. Who is he? Why does he hate your family, particularly? I suppose, he might well have reason..."

Her hands trembled and she looked at the floorboards, somehow feeling more like a foolish schoolgirl than a woman her age. She sat straighter and made an effort to look more bold, meeting his eyes, though they were only calm. He watched her patiently.

"Might I ask why you wish to know?"

"Because strange things have been happening. I'd like to know what I might attribute to whom."

He smiled. "Very well. You're only confirming my suspicions, by the way. Are you telling me that my son is not at peace?" She was pained for a moment. He saw this, then continued, "It's happened before. I wonder, sometimes, if our family line is especially susceptible to vampirism. It could be, we are killers ourselves. As for Bickerstaff, what I know is this. He came for me when I was a young man. I wounded him, but he escaped. He did not return until my boy attracted his notice. Nobody expected it then, because of his age. He appeared older than his seventeen years, so perhaps it was a mistake. Bickerstaff prefers to fight us in our prime, you see. My son narrowly survived the attack, due to our intervention. My grandfather survived him too. Later, Bickerstaff killed some of his siblings and my own father. Or so go the tales. When we fought, I asked him why he would not leave our family in peace. Bickerstaff froze, then answered, 'You cost me my family. You were part of a terrible betrayal.' He went on to explain the rest."

Miriam gasped, tightening her stole around her. Fox fur somehow seemed unremarkable compared to the wolf's fur on his collar. Perhaps he'd hunted it himself. She listened as he went on.

"It was a horrible fight. He was so strong, but in the end, I wounded him enough that he could not continue. If anything, he seemed impressed, thrilled. He dragged himself towards a wall and propped himself up. I was nursing my own wounds, you see. These... forgive me." He unbuttoned his shirt a little way, showing her the edges of some deep gashes, beginning at his sternum.

When she had taken it in, he covered himself again. "I knew he had been defeated, but I had to stop the bleeding, or I would not outlast him. He might even have been able to heal from the... from my blood. He told me that he had sworn to wipe out my bloodline, but I would be allowed to live. I knew he'd come for my sons. He even maimed my wife – I suppose she must have been fierce enough to attract his attention. Afterwards, though she survived, she was no longer a threat to him. Both her arm and her... innards had been damaged enough. We could have no more children."

Miriam gasped and covered her mouth with both hands. Varkov went on, "He told me he was from an extinct vampire clan named 'Star-Cross.' They sounded rather romantic in their way. They were the clan who arranged weddings between vampires. He said they were formed between... was it South Cross, an extinct clan, and Nightfall? We all know Nightfall." He rifled through his desk and pulled out a small volume. He read for a while, and then added, "Southern Cross. Slavers, like Death Rattle. Poachers, smugglers and drug peddlers. Southern Cross was destroyed, like Star-Cross, but the latter had gone with the support of the other clans. We know this for certain, as it's true that we played a part. Bickerstaff said that he was the last of Star-Cross, and that we had killed his entire clan and his beloved wife."

Miriam stared, wide-eyed. "How?"

Varkov chuckled. "Daylight helped us, another clan. It was led by a woman, would you believe it? Even if she let her husband, Daminh Gratina, steer their actions. St. Daminh was feeding information to us,as well as others like us. That legendary saint who wiped out entire clans from the inside out. He was a wonder, a miracle of God's providence. I can't tell you what it's like for us. The population in general think we are insane –mad – only because we know what they are and we've accepted that they exist. Every now and then, we have to dodge a murder charge, or deal with some other of their devices. The most powerful vampires aren't stupid. They'll use any means they can to uproot us. Direct violence is comparatively rare."

"If your son still lived?"

He watched her. "He knows. He's known since he was young what would happen if he lost and... was changed. We have all made a pact to die and not choose to kill. Its what revenants do, without exception. It's inevitable. They take human lives. We will hunt him down too."

Miriam covered her mouth with her hand, and took a few deep breaths. Somehow, she hadn't expected the harsh reality for them. "You'll kill him?" she gasped. "He's your son."

Alexander smiled. "I knew, as do we all. If we lose, we die. Do you know where my boy sleeps?"

Miriam let out a sound of disappointment and disgust. "I don't know... I'll tell you, though. Soon. If you don't find out before I do. Only, do I know everything about Bickerstaff, before I go back to Viola?"

Alexander chuckled. "There's no more to tell. From my grandfather's day until now, Bickerstaff has hunted us. The family stories make no difference. He dies, my son dies ... they are both dead already."

Miriam made it back to Whitby, feeling more disjointed than she had before she had left home. The sun was high, and she wandered along the promenade, doing nothing useful. She returned to her room as the storm rolled in.

Strictly speaking, she had to return to work, but it made little enough difference. If they paid her one half more, then she might care. As it was, as long as the books were up to date, she had a bit of leeway. If she had a few more clients like Carol, she'd do alright. She supposed Carol must have grown tired of being underpaid herself, as she was always fair.

Sinjen woke her at dusk. She'd been fully clothed on her bed, with her pillow over her face, trying to drown out the thunder.

"Bad news?" Sinjen enquired, stroking her ankle.

"They'll kill the poor boy. And... he says, Star-Cross? Supposedly, Bickerstaff is the sole survivor of that clan and has a vendetta. Um, excuse me, but which clan do you belong to?"

Sinjen raised an eyebrow as she rolled over and considered him. "I'm from Nightfall. The oldest and strongest clan. I'm... basically the runt, though."

"Then they must be very grand?" she asked, sounding a little more amazed than she'd intended.

Sinjen laughed. "I suppose they are. Did he tell you other horrors? There are many misconceptions about us."

She covered her face and could not look at him for a few moments. "You all kill, by obligation."

He chuckled. "I only feed on animal blood. I can even buy it. Is that satisfactory? I'd never kill anyone."

She studied him, a little puzzled. "That's true? Then why do the others kill?"

The corner of his lip curled slightly upwards. "Why do most humans eat meat? Why do they claim that they must feed in this way? Please excuse me, but, where I died, they only ate vegetables. They seemed to do well enough, a pinch rotund, if anything."

Miriam chuckled, "They really had so much food that they could grow fat off vegetables?"

Sinjen kissed her. "Let me take you to dinner. You deserve a proper meal. Have anything, it's quite alright, and don't complain."

The Pool Party

Chapter 17

Sinjen was away for a few nights afterwards, as he had to throw his party. Miriam was safe to watch over Varkov and Viola. Richard, too, would keep watch. Sinjen had sent another thrall to stay at the guest house to mind Alexander the fourth. The leader of Wolfsbane had been out with his clan to search for his son, but hadn't found him yet.

Jack was enjoying his new life. He'd been back to see Carol, and had given her more than enough that she might have retired. She had not, of course. He had done as instructed, and arranged everything Sinjen had asked, and Lord Marlais had had his pond prepared. Jack now wore his whip crossed over his chest; the carefully crafted design would deter even Carlotta, who had taken a bit of a shine to the man.

The party would be thrown at one of Lord Marlais' properties. This one was quite small compared to his usual accommodation, but had generous grounds and a natural pool built into it, filtered with reeds at the edges. The swimming lanes were brick and could get slimy, so he was happy it had been cleaned. Sinjen could stand in it, and the water was both natural and clear, though only vampires would want to make use of it in this season.

Jack dipped a toe in, watching the preparations, and shuddered violently at the thought of swimming in January. "July, sure, but why now?"

"We don't feel the cold, and the long nights are nice." Sinjen laughed. "No one, even our most delicate ladies, will mind the chill. But take care to do as I say, and have fires, blankets and spirits prepared to warm their dear unholy feet afterwards. At any rate, we'll keep it warmed a little, to take the edge off. Ice would spoil the mood."

Jack stared at him blankly for a moment, then shook his head to dismiss the ideas floating around in there. "May I come to the party?"

"You can. Only wear a ribbon with my personal seal around your neck so that they know you are my property and will not kill you. I don't want people getting confused. Your whip, too; you're so pretty with it."

"I'm... yours?" he asked, looking at his feet and hands.

"Can't you feel it?" Sinjen asked. "I'm only asking, I was never a thrall. In other circumstances, I might be a highly regarded type of creation. My maker, Amrita... She was clever and not unfair, only wicked if she... I can't express to you what it would mean to me if I could see her again. Just as a mother or father loves their child, a maker loves their offspring. It's harder still for an undead child to neglect or forget their parent. My dear mother did love me. I was a source of pride, however briefly. I remember the touch of her teeth, her bite, even more keenly than a baby would recall his mother's milk, or the softness and warmth of her breast. It's just not a pleasant memory." Jack recoiled, and Sinjen put his hand out to the man. "I can't explain it, I guess, but if I were to turn you, then you would be my blood. You'd never forget me."

Jack took hold of him and kissed him hard, to the alarm of the few men who were making preparations for his event. Sinjen had hired them for other parties, and they had seen enough by now not to look twice, but he recoiled from the touch of the whip.

"Do you hate me, now you have me?" Jack gasped, removing the whip and pulling him close again. "Your kisses feel like nothing tonight."

"I am nothing." Sinjen frowned. "I'm only property myself. Don't get attached, the odds of my survival are still low. If I die, by the way, would you go to find the Varkov family? It would be nice if someone avenged me. You can keep the whip."

Jack sighed and kissed him again. "You're in a melancholy mood."

Sinjen pressed his cheek against Jack's own. "I don't especially like men. Can you tell?"

Jack grinned, and kissed him again. "I can't tell."

That night the vampires gathered around the fires and pool. Sinjen was grinning, and a few vampires became visibly nervous, including Harry, who had not lowered his guard since their last fight. Sinjen went over to him and requested a dance as the band played. Harry consented, though he did not look comfortable. It was unusual for Sinjen to dance with a man; this was lost on no one.

Sinjen had been a little amused to see that they were still wary of him without Eliza there, even if they were in no immediate danger. Afterwards he found Sora, one of Harry's girls, and the two took a walk, not returning until Sora asked to swim.

Like a number of others, Sinjen stripped off and dove into the pool. His nudity counted for nothing, since he'd been enough of a spectacle over the years, along with his dear family.

Eliza too, tended to debase him in all the ways she could think of, quite often in front of other people. Even if he pretended to enjoy some of it. It wasn't enough for her until she'd seen suffering, and so he'd developed the perverse habit of pretending to enjoy what he did not, and of appearing to hate what he could tolerate enduring again.

He rested by the pool, wrapped in a bath towel, between a fire and the women in their pretty swimwear. Jack had come to join him, and he let the young man rest his head on his stomach, while the fire baked the water from his clothes. The steam swirled away, and was oddly satisfying to watch.

"Did you get a bit splashed?"

"A bit, lugging hot water around. I may have cooked a frog by accident," Jack admitted – he sounded sad about it. Sinjen chuckled.

Carlotta called to him, so he left Jack resting with his back to the flames, his head on a towel instead. Sinjen was still mostly nude, his skin having warmed next to the fire. He walked towards Carlotta, who was resting at the brick edge of the pool, one leg in the cold water.

"Sinjen. What have you done to my sweet Harry? He's in such a funny mood."

"He did it to himself, darling. Have you known one another long?"

Carlotta bit her lip and stroked his hair; it was almost dry again. "Yes. He was kind to me after I turned. He helped me to get established at Moonlight, before returning abroad. But why pick on him?"

"I wasn't, darling, he picked on me. He's jealous."

"Of what?" she asked. Her pretty green eyes sparkled, appearing gold and brown as they reflected his fires.

"Of you." He knelt and brushed a strand of hair from her face, then leant in and kissed her lips.

"You're too cruel," she sighed.

"I could be more cruel." He stroked the sides of her wet swim-dress and rolled it up.

"Get off me, Sinjen. How dare you?"

He smiled, kissed her on each cheek, and only continued to lift up her dress. Her legs kicked and her narrow hips wriggled away from him. He caught her and drew her closer. "Carlotta, I want you. Let me show them all what I feel."

"You can't, they'll know."

"They won't. It'll be stranger if I never have you, when I've had practically everyone else. Only I want you in front of everyone. You're mine, I want them to see."

She gasped and flailed, trying, without real effort, to push him away. He sighed and forced her arms upwards, holding them beneath his own. Kissing her, even as he felt some of the others watching with concern.

"Show them you want me, or I can't take you, my love. You're the only one who has ever meant anything to me."

He felt her gasp, her struggles lessen and her legs wrap around him. He'd pulled her swimsuit up above her belly button, everything above her cotton stockings was bare. Anyone could see her lower half, and his own nudity. He threw his towel over them both, suddenly a little protective.

"Tell me you want me," he whispered, pulling away, very slightly, even as she drew him closer with her legs.

"I want you," she gasped. "Sinjen."

He took her, pulling her short dress up to her ribs as he drove into her, then lifted her hips so that he could fill her totally. His breathing quickened. He could sense people watching. She was his woman, and an eternity might not change that. Harry would not, and he knew he couldn't do a thing about it.

"Carlotta," he sighed.

"Lady Carlotta," she returned, her breath catching. "Say it."

He did not, and only ploughed into her harder, then turned her over. Bending her, in front of everyone, at the edge of the pool, pinning her arms behind her back.

She called, "Sinjen, say it!"

"Lady Carlotta," he hissed. "Congratulations on your promotion, you awful harpy." He felt her tighten around him, and knew she'd been satisfied. "Isn't it enough that I have you? Did you need to make me envious right then?"

She was still trying to catch her breath. "I wanted both. I love you, Sinjen."

That was enough to satisfy him too, and they held one another.

"Excuse me, but may I have some too?" came a rich voice from the pool. Both Sinjen and Carlotta turned to see Tansy Darkwood. Sinjen laughed and let Carlotta go. She slipped away, tidying her clothes as he slid into the pool.

He'd never had Tansy's attention before, though he'd often admired her skin, like everyone else. Lightly freckled and milky white, the veins on her neck, and some at the side of her face, pale blue and clearly visible. She must have been a thrall once. Skin like that was a desirable trait, and had destroyed stronger vampires than him. He kissed her with trepidation, and made a mental note to eat and drink nothing while she was near. He'd heard enough about her not to let her close without caution.

"Tansy," he whispered, "I can't tell you how much I've wanted to touch your skin. I know I'm a fool for it."

She laughed prettily and a small blush came to her cheeks. "You remind me of someone. Conventional beauty like yours is such a bore, don't you think?"

"So I'm told," he agreed, lifting her out of the water and to the edge of the pool, where thin mud coated her thighs and backside.

"Then remind me why I love it," she whispered. In answer he pressed her knees up and apart, and demonstrated.

At some point in the small hours, when Sinjen had put some clothes on and sat drinking with Jack, Lord Marlais and Sora, Harry turned up for a few words. He beckoned Sinjen over, and Sinjen sent Jack back to the house. Though he'd been interesting to a lot of the vampires, he wasn't willing to leave him at the party unattended. The event had gone very well, at least for everyone except Harry. As a consequence, most of the vampires were not at their most inhibited.

As Sinjen followed him into Marlais' hedge maze, he thought he'd better say something. "Look, I know that was below the belt, but you and she aren't actually together, are you?"

Harry's back stiffened. "No. That's not what's been bothering me. I don't expect I'll get anywhere with Carlotta for a while. Even if I do have some merits, they usually take time to become apparent, or so I'm told. It did sting a bit, though."

"Would it make you feel better if I told you she waited until that moment to tell me she outranks me now?" he volunteered.

Harry grinned at him. "It does a bit. I've been thinking... this fledgling."

"From what I've been told, it's fair to say he isn't likely to last," Sinjen admitted.

"So what should I do? Do you still want me to make arrangements for him?"

"I do. We'll save him if we can."

Harry turned to him and asked, "What are you planning? I really don't want any involvement with this, and I won't take kindly to being pushed into a fight with that particular family, or that particular rogue. Are you really planning to kill him?"

"Isn't there a reasonable chance that those two problems might cancel each other out with very minimal effort?" Sinjen suggested. "It might even be possible to claim his bounty. What's needed, head or heart?"

Harry sighed. "It's a ring. He should be wearing a red ring, it should do as proof, but you won't get it. It's not going to happen."

"I don't understand what the difficulty is, Harry," Sinjen said, now walking at his side. "Between us, it can't be impossible. Is he older than you?"

Harry raised an eyebrow. "Good heavens, no. I should think he's somewhere around your age; no, a generation older."

"I was told his age was estimated at three hundred."

"Ah, these vampire slayers do like to exaggerate, don't they?"

"Why are we taking a scenic walk through Marlais' maze? I'm just going to assume he kills people here too..." Sinjen asked, a little nervously.

Harry laughed. "Because it's a quiet place to talk. Oh, and I had a letter, or rather you did. I intercepted it, because I'm supposed to, but it was a little bit puzzling so I thought I'd get your opinion on it."

He took a small scroll out of his jacket pocket and handed it to Sinjen. It read:

My correspondent is rather lax in her messages of late and, with Moonlight so busy, I grow restless.

The message had been written on a ripped fragment of parchment paper, rolled up, and sealed with a button of silver wax and a thumbprint.

"I can guess who sent that, and what kind of threat is represented," Harry explained. "But how much danger would you be in if I handed that over to Eliza?"

"A great deal, but if you really must do this, then hand it over to her. I won't be blackmailed over it. He does exactly what he wants, doesn't he?"

"Sinjen, something like this could trigger an entire investigation. Especially as he gave you his verdict not so long ago. It might be considered a contributing factor."

Sinjen sighed. "Look, it's not all that, but I admit I would rather avoid the trouble. What do you want? Money?"

Harry chuckled. "I want two things, and yes, some money wouldn't hurt, but that's irrelevant. The first thing is this: a dear friend tells me I need to appear reliable, and more like him, to impress my lady. So, naturally, the easiest way to do this is to get *him* to make me appear this way."

Sinjen motioned for him to continue.

"The second thing is that I should clear the air with you, my afore-mentioned friend. So, I need to tell you something. Therefore, I need you to promise that you won't be angry with me."

"Oh. I know what this is." Sinjen sighed, exhausted. "Tell me, then."

"It was me. She was just so pretty, Sinjen. What was I supposed to do?" Harry admitted.

Sinjen took a deep and shuddering breath. "I'm..."

"Look, such a pure-hearted beauty, weeping at me and telling me that she had to be with her love. One who had alre—"

"Harry."

"I know," Harry said, wincing. "That's why we're out of the way, and why I tested you earlier. Just, at least don't bring Eliza into it."

Sinjen was still too angry to talk and motioned to the exit of the maze. That path led out to the front entrance, where most of the vehicles had been parked.

Seeing that it wasn't going very well, Harry decided to go all in with a flurry of excuses.

"You'd already abandoned her once and you were already screwed, but I couldn't tell either of you. I didn't think you'd still be around at this point. I just didn't want her to suffer more. At least I kept her out of Daylight, and you had a few short month—" He had to stop talking, as all of the air had been knocked out of his lungs. Sinjen had hit him, not with the normal weight of his body, but with something like the force of a charging bull. For a moment Harry couldn't see properly, except to dodge a pale shape hurtling towards him again. His back was sliced open, and he had to spirit a distance away to get a clear view.

He landed on the other side of the cars, then realised his mistake. "Oh shit," he breathed, watching the Nightfall spirit form approach.

If it had had wings, he'd already be upon him, but the reptilian monstrosity he saw wasn't much better. Sinjen walked up to Harry's car and lifted it over his head. Harry shouted for help, as Sinjen let out an inhuman roar and threw the car at him. Harry barely had time to slip into mist before it passed through him. He felt claws as Sinjen grabbed him and pulled him back into shape. He reformed, in terrible pain, still trying to get free.

Sora's maroon Nightfall form grappled Sinjen's arms and wrestled him off. She was smaller than Sinjen, but faster, and a trained knight. Harry tried to help her, but realised he was too injured to fight. He heard Marlais laugh as Harry was struck hard and collapsed, losing consciousness. He looked up in time to see Lord Marlais' own apelike spirit form, smiling and clinging to Sinjen's back. His narrow arms and sharp claws were wrapped around the younger vampire's throat.

Seeking Alliances

Chapter 18

S injen's eyes opened to see Jack first, wiping his brow with a damp cloth. He turned to the window, though his neck felt like it was burning. He could see, by the still darkening sky, that it was the next night.

Jack was looking at his throat with concern. Sinjen probed the area. He could move, so the injury was manageable.

"What on earth did you think you were playing at?" Sora said, striding into the room. She had not long woken herself.

"How's Harry?" Sinjen asked, sitting up with care and going to look at his injuries in the mirror. He'd lost strips of skin from his neck last night, and what felt like a great deal of blood too; he was dizzy. His wrists, also, were very bruised.

Sora sat on the edge of the bed, crossed her legs and leant back, looking very irritated. "Do you have any idea what a headache this will be for me?" she complained. "Not only did you manage to learn..."

"Can we hush it up?" Sinjen asked.

"You need to ask Harry. Marlais thought it was very amusing. He's all in favour of it, though I don't doubt he'll tell Eliza. You almost killed Harry, though, and if he wants to make an issue of it then we can't do anything. For myself, I'd sooner avoid inquisitors and investigations. Most of the guests were too inebriated to see, or care, what you did by then, anyway. Only Darkwood saw that form for certain, and I expect Carlotta will be able to convince her to ignore the matter. It's not like it involves her, she's only here to see Marlais really."

"Where is Harry, then?" Sinjen asked.

"His room, being minded by Carlotta." Sora flopped back and gave him a look which clearly indicated she wasn't being paid enough for the trouble he was causing her. He flicked her lightly on the nose as he went out.

"Is he really alright?" he heard Jack ask as he left.

Sinjen listened at Harry's door before he went in. He could hear Carlotta giving him a piece of her mind. "I told you not to tell him. Can you please assume I know what I'm talking about, even some of the time? At least when it comes to Sinjen!"

"Well, he had to find out sooner or later, didn't he? I couldn't have that hanging over my head forever. He was quite agreeable, really."

He heard Carlotta let out a hiss of frustration. "He fractured your spine in three places. How was he reasonable? You could have died, and you'd better hope he's not still angry."

"I think he kind of knew already, darling. How many of us could you have influenced as you did?" Harry asked, unconcerned.

"Don't blame me! You— You were the elder, you might have—"

"I might have ignored you? Assumed you didn't know what you were talking about?" Harry asked.

Carlotta huffed, and he heard her walk to the window. "You might have told me more than you did," she finished.

Sinjen tapped on the door, and pushed it open after a moment. Carlotta was sitting by the window, glaring at him. Harry was lazing on his bed, with his arms behind his head and one foot resting on his knee.

"I feel a bit calmer now. Are you alright?" Sinjen asked, walking over to him.

"I don't know, Sinjen. I might die, and the wound to my heart—"

"I'll buy you a new car."

"I suppose I'll recover in time. Though my poor bones..."

"And I'll get you a special treat just to make it up to you, my dear brave boy," Sinjen said, rolling his eyes.

"It's lucky I have a spare car."

"Men are very queer," Carlotta said with a sigh, then got up and left the room. She could see that neither of them would speak seriously if she was there.

Harry sat up and stroked Sinjen's neck. "That wasn't me, you know."

"Yes, I remember."

"I would have thought twice about telling you, if I'd known you'd taught yourself that spirit form. Carlotta said you play your cards close to your chest, but I didn't see that coming."

"I have a lot of cards, Harry," Sinjen said, folding his arms over Harry's chest and laying his head over them. Harry brushed his hair from his eyes.

"Was that a serious attempt on my life?" he asked.

"Why did Carlotta wake up alone in a forest? What were you thinking?"

Harry sighed. "Oh, that. I was there, I didn't leave her alone. It's only that the cemetery was surrounded by so much wild garlic. I think that's why it happened. I found her fairly quickly, but she was terrified in the meantime. I wasn't really in Italy. I lied about that, for obvious reasons."

"Do you have any idea how much that image haunted me?" Sinjen said, and Harry stroked his hair again, thinking he might cry.

"I promise she was alright afterwards. That was the only hiccup. I didn't foresee it happening; it took me years to work out that it had likely been the flowers."

To his surprise Sinjen put his arms around him and actually did cry. Harry sat up and held him. "You actually do love her."

"Look, it's complicated. Don't think there's anything for you to worry about."

"You'll do what you promised?" Harry asked.

"Yes, but keep quiet about this, and your side of things."

"Of course. In that case, I think neither of us will have anything to worry about. I'm still not helping you with Victor's bounty. I haven't changed my mind on that."

"You know, I kind of like when you stroke my hair," Sinjen said.

"It *is* soft... but get off me. We need to eat, and I suspect we should check on your Miriam."

"Alright then, I'll meet you in an hour."

Harry sighed. "I'd ask why, except I'll have to arrange transport anyway."

Sinjen grinned at him and left.

They were still at Lord Marlais' house, and out of courtesy Sinjen went to see Marlais and apologise for causing a scene.

Marlais was trimming his beard. He'd already shaped and waxed his moustache. "Oh no. Don't worry at all. I was bemoaning the lack of excitement, if anything. I've never seen someone throw a car before, either. Are they very heavy?" he asked conversationally, wiping some hair off his scissors.

"They are. I apologise for the lack of guests, too. I didn't bother trying to convince mortals to come for a swim in the middle of January."

Marlais chuckled. "You didn't have to mention the pool at all, dear Sinjen, but never mind. There will be other parties. I enjoyed myself anyway. Sometimes a change can be quite nice."

"Thank you, Lord Marlais." Sinjen turned to leave, not wanting to disturb him further, but he was called back.

"I was wondering, actually, how are you finding your time away from Lady Eliza? You've been out a great deal, I noticed."

"It's been quite novel. So many things have changed in recent years, and though it seems like there are more diversions than ever, I almost can't remember what to do with this much time to myself. Not that Eliza *never* gives me my own time, of course."

"Of course," Marlais said, and there was a note of danger in his voice. "However, if you have any difficulty filling your time in the usual way, then I'm happy to assist you."

"Yes. I did notice I was missing a bit more skin than I'd have expected," Sinjen said, touching his neck, as Marlais pulled his cut-throat razor from his bag. Marlais smiled cheerfully at him, and indicated that he could go.

Sinjen went downstairs to the servants' quarters and made a phone call to Lord Petri's offices. A gruff-voiced man answered and asked which service he required. Sinjen explained he had questions about a bounty.

His call was transferred elsewhere, and a very bored-sounding woman answered, "Bounties Department. How can I assist Nightfall today?"

"I need to know about an unusual contract that I've heard of. The proof required is a red ring. Do you know which rogue that might refer to?"

He could hear papers shuffling, though he knew that any Penumbra agent would likely know every possible bounty, and especially any with odd details. "I'm sorry, sir. There is no contract for a rogue fitting that description. Will there be anything else today?"

Sinjen resisted the urge to sigh audibly. The poor girl was clearly being difficult just for some amusement, or possibly had not yet had breakfast. "Are there any bounties at all requiring or requesting a ring as proof?"

"There was one, Mr. Carlyle, but it has long expired. There is another that may be relevant, but it is with lost objects. Would you like to be transferred?"

"Go on then," he said, looking at his watch. "Would you also mind explaining the query to the next person? I don't want to get them mixed up."

She made an affirmative sound, and, to his surprise, after a few moments he heard Lord Petri's deep and slightly melodic voice answer. "My ring, Mr. Carlyle. Has it turned up?"

"Oh, no, Elder Petri. It's just that I've heard an interesting connection to it recently, so I was phoning for information on the story, and if it is known who might have it."

"How disappointing," Elder Petri said, his tone too professional for any real trace of emotion to ring through. He did sound, perhaps, a little more sombre than usual. "The ring belonged to my... my clan. It was given as part of a dowry, for a wedding arranged by Star-Cross. Back in the days when we still had formal marriages. This was a personal gift, you understand, from me to a dear friend who had little at the time. Though both have survived until today, the ring was stolen. This happened on its way to Asia, as it was transported by Southern Cross and Death Rattle. There was an ambush, and the ring was believed to have been among the treasures stolen by vampire hunters.

It was last held by the Varkov family, who use a wolf as their sigil, and who, I believe, are still the leaders of the Wolfsbane Sect to this day. It has not been seen for at least a century, and may have been sold or lost. It was very valuable. Is that information of any use to you? If the ring is found, I am still very much willing to pay for its return. Its value and sentimental worth are considerable to me."

"Thank you for your time, Lord Petri. I'll let you know if I hear anything further about the matter," Sinjen said, and Petri hung up.

He stretched and went to see Harry, who had by now had a carriage prepared for them. Sinjen was very glad to see it, not only because Marlais kept all his vehicles and horses in perfect order, but because Harry wouldn't be driving.

Sinjen sat next to him, delighted, and Harry correctly guessed the reason. "Remember to get a few bicycles too, when you go to look for a new automotive, and a couple of extras for Lady Eliza's guests. Actually, I wonder if she'd like a car too?" Sinjen frowned. "That could be a terrible idea. Never mind, she would tell me if she wanted one."

Harry coughed politely.

"Yes, charge them to me. I was just asking Lord Petri about his ring, but the phone call wasn't overly helpful, except that he mentioned Southern Cross and Death Rattle lost it in an ambush. I don't suppose you know much about that?"

"Mmm. Rings a bell," Harry said, looking at the window instead of at him. "I haven't seen dear Emma in quite a few days, I wonder if she's feeling better?"

"Your sickly mistress?" Sinjen said, casting him a sidelong glance.

"Indeed. That poor girl. You know, when she's just come out of a coughing fit, she really is rather beautiful. Her dear little hands tremble so, and she lets me hold her tiny little wrists."

Sinjen touched his neck, thinking that the last thing he would want to see today was a small and narrow hand. He hadn't eaten anything like enough, and superficial injuries took longer to heal. "Well. Hopefully she's been all the better for your short absence."

Harry sighed. "I'd like more time with her, I really would, but this one was on her last legs even before I found her. I'll be so bitterly disappointed if the reaper took her while I was away. I did hire an excellent nurse for her, but even that dear woman felt she was rather hopeless."

"I see. So, it's the mathematics that concerns you."

Harry nodded slowly. "And I am rather hungry, after my injuries, Sinjen."

"Well, you could feed before you see her." They were approaching the narrow stretch of road where they had fought not long ago, and he couldn't be bothered to argue any more. Sinjen had put on a soft scarf, but resented having to wear it actually wrapped around his neck, given the number of times, including last night, that he'd been strangled. Still, Miriam couldn't be allowed to see the marks – what would she think?

"Honestly, Sinjen. Do you even fixate? That's like offering a man a bowl of cold porridge when all day he's been looking forward to a beef roast with all the trimmings. I can't just turn it off, do I really need to explain it? What kind of vampire are you?"

Sinjen frowned. "We aren't all the same. Arthur—"

"Arthur has his own type of fixation. He still feeds on death, but what do you do? I've never actually been able to find out; even Carlotta isn't sure."

"Don't gossip, Harry. It's not proper."

Harry grinned and elbowed him lightly. "Want to swap stories?"

"I think we've grown quite close enough for now," Sinjen said, looking out of the window in a low, contemplative mood.

He heard Harry sigh. "Look, whatever it is, it doesn't make you any less a vampire."

Sinjen shot him a look of irritation. His eyes and voice had become cold again. "You *know* what it is that interests me, Harry, better than most people."

Harry straightened in his chair, his eyes widening for a moment, before he too turned to the window. The carriage was now descending the hill towards the sea. It was a pretty view.He stuck his head out to see better, and looked happy enough that Sinjen couldn't help smiling a little. "You're like a dog or something."

"My aunts always used to tell me so," Harry admitted with a sheepish grin, one which turned to sadness as he returned to the view. "A shame I wasn't more obedient, I suppose."

Sinjen patted his knee absently.

"They'd have loved you," Harry continued, "You'd have been a perfect little prince in their eyes, I don't doubt. I suppose I was for long enough... or, perhaps I only looked the part. Did you have a lot of women in your family?"

"It was just me and my sisters, and the cousin you saw, after a point."

"Ah, that's the proper way around. Not with them in charge of everything to do with you. I suppose you were the breadwinner," Harry said, resituating himself and looking at Sinjen with interest.

"We'd been left a little by our parents, enough to carry on well enough; after that, fate was good to us. In retrospect, perhaps I took my freedom the moment I could. It was... not a burden, really, but a lot of responsibility," he replied, looking at the rows of little houses they passed. One of which, hopefully, still contained his fledgling.

"Then, I suppose we have that in common, at least," Harry said, smiling sadly at him.

Whelks on Toast

Chapter 19

Miriam was waiting for him in the cafe again. She smiled as she saw him enter, and beckoned him over.

"A new book?" he asked. "Oh no, are you bored of vampires now?"

She giggled. "This one has pirates. Though I'm not sure I want to meet one of those either."

"You have. Harry was one, I think, at least at one point. Then again, it's Harry – he's a little workshy. Can I order some pastries for us?"

"I've been eyeing the Eccles cakes," Miriam suggested, "they look rather good today. This pot of tea is fresh, so just ask for another teacup."

Sinjen smiled and bought the cakes. They were still warm and the sugared pastry sparkled in the light. The Christmas tree had been taken down, so they had more space at Miriam's usual table, even if the room was a little more plain now. "At first, I didn't realise that the paper lanterns were only decorative. I wonder if they'd like some string lights, they could be rather cheerful."

Miriam looked up at them; they were only hung on the ceiling, and there were a few small ones on the tables. "I didn't notice them. You'd think the table ones would be a fire hazard. They don't really seem necessary, and the tables aren't very big to start with."

"Mere appendix?" Sinjen suggested. Miriam frowned at him, but topped up his tea. This was a black tea, especially dark – it had a surprisingly pleasant aroma of rich earth. He'd have to ask what kind it was. "Does the cafe seem a little bit nicer?"

"I might have made a small investment in it," Miriam admitted. "Maybe the lights would be nice, if they aren't expensive to run."

Sinjen smiled affectionately. "You're really rather precious."

She looked at him like she wasn't sure if that was a compliment or not, but satisfied herself that, by his expression, it was. "Viola is doing alright. I see her during the day, but it's getting risky. Yesterday, I saw a vampire hunter and quite toppled the poor woman into a shrub to conceal her. He saw me, but I only introduced myself, and let him follow me elsewhere. Viola forgave me, don't worry."

Sinjen chuckled. "How did you know he was a hunter?"

"He was quite conspicuous. He was heavily scarred, and I believe carried one of those walking sticks which are really swords; at least, it was clinking a little when he walked. He did look rather dashing, actually. I can well understand how Viola..." She trailed off at the look Sinjen was giving her but then picked up again. "Considering how perfect-looking their targets are, you'd think you'd allow them their own dangerous sort of charm," she almost scolded.

Sinjen looked out of the window and, slightly theatrically, objected, "Well, perhaps I thought you might favour one type over another."

Miriam was unimpressed, and kicked him lightly under the table. He took her arm, and they began to make their way down to the pier.

It was a clear, starry night, but the waves were fierce. There was a stronger tide than usual, influenced by the new moon. He recounted to her what he had learnt about the ring and bounty.

"Are vampires really affected by the tides and flooded rivers?" Miriam asked, distracted by the crashing waves.

"Not exactly. It is easier to cross a flooded river, though. I've always wondered if that might be because it would be full of run-off from graves, or even perhaps there could be bodies in the water? I'm not sure how we would determine that exactly, but I was once at a place where I knew there would be human remains in the river. It was as easy to cross there as when they are in flood. It's not totally impossible otherwise, it's just very unpleasant. Unless you are a ghoul or an unblooded fledgling of course, then it can't be done."

"Then you must have drunk blood," Miriam pointed out.

"Alright, it would be unwise to have never done it," Sinjen confessed.

"But, when you say unblooded, you must really mean…"

"Yes, I've killed someone," Sinjen said, frowning.

"What about the tides?" Miriam said, encircling herself with her arms, not sure if she wanted to know any more.

"I think that's only a misunderstanding. It's painful to cross the sea, but there are some places, because we are also spirits, that affect us greatly. Like crossroads, a place between many places, or between different kinds of environments can be very disorienting for us. A number of those locations are by the coast, particularly if there are dramatic swathes of sand, and the tides can help us to leave if we are lost there, buried, perhaps – it's not an everyday problem. We can get a better sense of direction by watching them. I'm not sure how to explain that fully. Some parts of the land can be kind of magical, and hold their own power."

"Is there some place like that here?" she asked.

"Yes, up there where the Abbey is. There's sea, the curve of the beach, the steep cliffs and the flat land where the monks lived, and then behind it is a lake and all almost circled by the path that leads to it. Such a place has a lot of power and... oh."

"Yes?"

"That's why Alexander ended up so far from his grave."

Miriam looked up at the Abbey. "I suppose holy people might know how to choose a good spot. Perhaps they're more sensitive to these things."

She was thinking about Viola's guest house. It was similar in some ways, between the cliffs and headland, leading sharply onto the moors. If she wasn't mistaken, they had also passed a crossroads not far from the house. She didn't know if the little well-loved garden had any of its own power, but she had seen a hothouse and what looked like a small crypt on the land. She had seen all of these things, but hadn't considered them in detail.

"This ring – I wonder if I should ask about it. I told Alexander senior that I'd tell him where his son was. I don't know if I really should or not. What do you think?"

Sinjen frowned. "Maybe it's better to stay away from that side of things."

"I'm not sure," Miriam admitted. "I think there might be danger in—"

"Yes, there is danger," a deep voice with a foreign inflection called from behind them. "You might step away from that man, Miss. He's not what he appears."

Sinjen turned around to see the hunter Miriam had described. Sinjen leant against the iron railings and took in his long blond hair and collection of scars. "Oh, I see what you mean about dangerous charm. I didn't expect him to look quite so noble, though. The collars are a bit of a uniform, I suppose. Who are you?"

The hunter grimaced. "Miss. You really should step away from him; they have been known to take hostages when threatened."

"I would never," Sinjen said, sounding affronted. "But you can't be planning to attack a gentleman in the middle of town, people would think you're barking mad. We can go somewhere else to fight later, if you really insist. I'm Sinjen Carlyle. Will you introduce yourself, please?"

The hunter looked a little bit irritated. "I'm Sergiu Ardelean, of Wolfsbane."

"Romanian, I guess?" Sinjen asked. "Well, it's very sweet of you to worry about my dear friend, but as you can see, we are only enjoying the view."

"I'm not in the habit of letting vampires enjoy their evenings."

Sinjen sighed. "Well, I did say I'd fight you, if you'd really like me to."

Ardelean paused for a moment. He had kept his cane in his hands throughout the exchange. "I heard what you said, Miss...?"

"Miriam Green," she supplied.

"We need to find our brother. We all swore an oath to the same end. If he has any honour he won't try to escape it. If it's any consolation, this duty will bring us no joy, and much pain. Where is he?"

Miriam looked between Sinjen and the hunter. "What should I do?" she asked Sinjen.

"Do what you think you should do."

The hunter's brow furrowed. "Are you enthralled by him?"

Miriam blushed. "I mean— I guess he's fairly charming, but why on earth?"

Sinjen laughed quietly and the hunter rolled his eyes. Sinjen pushed her lightly towards Ardelean, who instructed her to hold out her hand. She did so. He pressed a silver cross, studded with pearls, into her palm. His mouth moved in wordless prayer before he placed the cross back around his neck. He looked puzzled, and did not let Miriam return to Sinjen but drew her alongside him instead. "Miss Green, no good can come of associating with these creatures, I caution you."

"Well, thank you," Miriam said, politely.

Ardelean was beginning to look more and more put out. He relaxed a little, and took a deep breath before he spoke again. "This is not much fun. But I have a duty. Lady, help me find my friend. He was impulsive, but he was not a monster. I don't wish him to live as one, even if he will not choose to leave his woman. I... I knew her too. I had hoped that they would be allowed to marry, and I saw his pain when she was gone, but please, this is a matter of lives, not hearts. There are always mistakes when it comes to love, but I can't let them make more now."

Sinjen raised an eyebrow at his words. He could see that Harry was on a roof nearby. As few people were around, he flipped over the rail and onto the staircase below them, spiriting to Harry when he was out of view.

Miriam spun around, frightened to suddenly find herself alone. Ardelean instantly became more at ease.

He took Miriam's arm, leading her to a pub along the seafront. The same one where Sinjen had befriended Jack.

The pub was rowdy and smelled of cigarette smoke and stale beer. Miriam wasn't an expert, but she had a suspicion that a number of the patrons might be dangerous people. Though weatherbeaten and tanned, they wore more than the usual amount of finery. They might be thieves, smugglers, even retired pirates. Her new companion was even more suspicious, if anything. He had looked rather grand outside, but in this setting, he fit in just as well, somehow. She noticed a few men checking out his valuables. They sized him up and lost interest, like they thought better of the idea.

He sat down and waved at an oversized man at the bar. The bartender finished putting a few bottles on a shelf behind him and lumbered out, with an unimpressed frown on his face.

"A couple of beers. Sorry, did you want beer?" Ardelean asked.

"Beer is fine," Miriam squeaked. It didn't look like it had occurred to Ardelean that she might have wanted something else.

"Do you have food?" he asked, looking around at the establishment as if for the first time.

Big Dave raised his eyebrows. "Can do you a pork pie, whelks on toast, or some potato crisps."

The hunter glanced at Miriam, then requested the crisps. When they were brought over, he asked if they were sea salt.

"We live by the sea. What do you think?" Dave said, and returned to the bar.

"Are you religious?" Ardelean asked, as Miriam took one.

"No, not... not especially."

"You should be. Where are your parents?" he asked, tersely.

"Can suicides become vampires?" she asked, ignoring the question, though he drew the connection anyway.

"It's not very likely, but it can happen. Odds are you'd have noticed by now, if someone in your family was one. Don't worry about that. I only advised you towards faith, as it would be wise if you plan on remaining near these monsters."

"He said they're quite interested in the Dracula tourism."

The hunter nodded. "They have a strong tendency towards self-obsession, but it's best if you don't encourage or engage with them. Ninety-nine times out of a hundred they have malintent."

"So, one in a hundred times, they might not?" she asked.

"That's woman logic. Think with your brain instead."

Miriam scowled at him. He turned to Dave and pointed to his drink. Dave got an especially large glass out from behind the bar and lifted it questioningly. Ardelean nodded. Neither of them wanted to be disturbed much, by the look of it.

"Should you be doing that if there are vampires abroad?" Miriam couldn't resist asking.

He smiled. "I fight better a little drunk. But, my brother."

She thought for a few moments. When she looked up, he'd already downed a quarter of his beer. Seeing her expression, he shrugged and said he was thirsty.

"The best I can do is bring him a message for you. You should choose a place to meet tomorrow and I'll ask him if he will join you there. I don't want to be responsible for a murder."

The vampire hunter nodded, but said, "Letting him live will be a surer way to be responsible for murder, I warn you."

Miriam looked at her own drink. She squeezed the handle of the metal mug a couple of times, considering her words.

"And there is no way to murder a dead man, only to put their souls to rest. They are all already dead," he added.

Seeing that their meeting was concluding, the hunter named his place. Miriam only warned him, if she was followed again, she would not pass on the message. He nodded, so she downed the rest of her drink and left.

She wandered down to the beach, expecting that Sinjen would find her there. He did, accompanied by Harry. Sinjen asked for the details, but Harry wandered away. She watched him pick up a good-sized cuttlefish bone and wander around looking for a few more.

The Tea Party

Chapter 20

S injen spirited Miriam to his townhouse, to decrease the chance they would be followed. He'd had to do it more than once, so made his excuses when he arrived and said he would not go in with her. Miriam was in his arms, and as her face was so close to his neck, he wasn't surprised when she pulled his scarf aside to expose his injuries. He was too tired at that moment to object. To his surprise, she did not ask what had happened to him, and only went inside. He walked off, wondering if that was better or worse.

Nobody was around, so he risked spiriting further away, very aware that he would be at risk if a hunter was around. He was starting to get annoyed with the futility of his search, when he finally saw a woman fastening her curtains. He waved at her and cast a glamour which would compel her to take an interest in him. She opened her window and asked if he was alright.

"Excuse me, ma'am, but I've taken a wrong turn. Do you know the way back?"

She closed the window. He waited a minute while she came out through the back door of her house and spoke to him from behind a wooden garden gate.

He approached, and carried on the conversation until he'd managed to fascinate her enough that she could be persuaded to leave her property, to point out the path she'd told him to take. He'd had to pretend to have poor vision before she would. When she stepped out, he took her in his arms, letting her struggle a little before he felt her resistances ebb away. He bit her throat, and had to make an effort to stop himself from killing her, but was so happy to have found food that he couldn't help but kiss her afterwards. He compelled her to forget the experience and go to bed.

He pressed his forehead against her fence and felt his injuries heal. He'd been a fool not to have eaten earlier. When he had recovered, he retreated to a roof to look for someone else.

This area was still very quiet, but Sinjen soon saw Miriam hurrying back towards town. She looked pale, and wiped her eyes a few times. Then she stopped and, remembering that she was in the far north of Whitby, turned around and ran back the way she had come. He could only think of one place she might be going, so followed her at a distance.

She didn't make it the whole way, instead stopping at a bench along one of the paths and throwing herself down onto it, collapsing into uncontrollable sobbing. He lit himself a cigarette and watched for a couple of minutes while she got the worst of it out of her system. Seeing that she was quite inconsolable, he did not finish it before spiriting to the bench and putting one hand on her back. The other still held his cigarette.

She sat up hurriedly and wiped her eyes, but when she tried to explain what was wrong, she could not. Sinjen pushed her head down onto his lap and stroked her hair until she'd recovered enough to speak.

She was still lying on him as she tried to explain again. "I can do it tomorrow. I can't ask you."

"Ask what, Miriam?" he said patiently, and lit a second smoke. He offered her a little, but she shook her head.

"Alexander said he would go and meet them, though Viola was... she was devastated, but she didn't really show it. I mean, she was careful to conceal her feelings. She almost fainted at one point. He sat her down and looked at her face like he was trying to never forget it. She was weeping; he kissed her. Then he turned to me and just shattered my heart."

Sinjen stroked her hair and waited. Miriam's voice had cracked a few times and she was trying not to cry again. "He only asked to meet his son before he died. I hadn't even realised that he'd never met him."

Sinjen took a deep drag and exhaled slowly. "That is rather distressing. I'm sorry, I should have gone with you."

She sat up and wiped her eyes. "You had to eat. Didn't you?"

"I didn't kill anyone, but yes," he said.

"Did you really think I was such an idiot that I'd believe the lie you told me. Have you lied about other things?"

"Not really."

"Why did you lie about that, then?" she snapped, tired from the whole ordeal.

"I didn't think you needed the worry, and... I didn't want to admit to it at that moment."

"Well, that was stupid, because I was worrying about why you thought I was an idiot instead."

He frowned. "Sorry."

"I get to choose what I can handle, not you. Okay?"

Sinjen considered her carefully. Her expression was hurt, angry and determined. Her eyes shone very brightly, their colour more vivid than before her tears. "Come on, I'll take you to my cottage. Let's get you warmed up, and I'll go and pass that information on to the hunter."

"Is that alright?"

"Yes. I need to eat again anyway." He pulled her up and kissed her, then let her look at his neck again.

"What *did* happen?"

"I got into a fight with Harry, and another vampire half killed me. It's fine now, though."

She frowned. "I thought he was your friend."

"He is," Sinjen said, and kissed her again. She only shook her head and leant against him.

Richard Wright let them in, delighted to see them both. As before, the house was very warm, but this time it seemed more cared for. There were a few bunches of early wildflowers, winter greenery and berries, arranged in vases and dotted around the place. The little cottage had also been cleaned and refreshed. Sinjen smiled to see it.

"Are you baking again?" he asked.

"Fisherman's pie," Richard said, glancing back at the kitchen.

Sinjen grinned, and instructed that a bed be prepared for Miriam. This time she didn't argue, she was too tired. Richard poured her a glass of white wine and disappeared into the kitchen to bring her a proper meal.

"I'd offer you some, sir, but it does have garlic in it," Richard said in apology.

"Quite alright. I won't be back until late tonight. I'll sleep here, though."

Richard nodded, and Sinjen slipped away into the night.

He arrived at the beach, a spot which was not usually overlooked at night, and walked to the pub where he'd spent New Year. It was a little more gritty than he remembered, but lively. The hunter was there, facing the door. Big Dave looked at Sinjen like he was remembering a particularly nasty hangover, and slammed a bottle of whiskey down on the bar. Sinjen grinned, took it over to Ardelean and poured them a glass each.

"I have a message," Sinjen began, his tone entirely polite, and lit another cigarette. "Do you mind if I smoke?"

"What's the message?"

Sinjen smiled, but couldn't help antagonising him a little. "Shouldn't you be a little nicer? Aren't you the good guys?"

"What's the message?" he repeated, and took a sip of his drink.

"Ah, it's very depressing. Can I ask you something first?"

He didn't answer so Sinjen continued, "Do you know anything about a red ring? It belonged to an important vampire, but was taken when

Daylight was still around. Afterwards, it might have ended up with your sect."

"No. Is he refusing to meet us?" the hunter asked.

"No. I said it was really sad, didn't I?" Sinjen laughed.

"That seems like a lot more sympathy than you usually have for one another. Would you like a whelk?"

Sinjen picked up the bowl and sniffed it cautiously.

"I think they're only boiled in saltwater," Ardelean clarified, "the toast is buttered." He indicated to Big Dave that they would like another, and one more bowl was brought out. Dave was looking especially irritated, but brightened the instant Sinjen and Ardelean threw some coinage down on the table.

Dave took the toast and old bowls away, and promised them better, hot toast instead. He also fetched them over two much nicer glasses, and tableware.

"Why did you ask me about a ring?" Sergiu Ardelean asked.

"Ah, just some vampire gossip, I suppose. There's money in it, so if it turns up, let me know."

Ardelean looked up at him. "We do accept leads and pay."

Sinjen smiled. "I've heard that too." He unbuttoned his shirtsleeve and showed Sergiu his Daylight brand.

"You should have led with that. Traditionally, we haven't accepted contracts against Daylight members, but I understood that they were—"

"Yes. There are only two of us who survived. Both of us have very little freedom. It's always good to make friends though, isn't it?" Sinjen disembowelled a large whelk quite contently, and looked up to see Big Dave walking towards them, with hot toast and an icebox. "You're spoiling us."

"Don't you love us any more, Davy?" called a man in some old-fashioned finery.

"Never liked you lot," Dave said. That table fell about laughing and making jokes.

"So, this bad news," Ardelean asked, seriously.

"He'll meet you, but he's never seen his son and he wants to meet him first," Sinjen said with a frown.

Pain flitted across the hunter's face. "We can do that. Best not baby them anyway, it's better if he sees, really. He's a sweet boy. Very like his father at that age, but too gentle at present for our line of work. His mother is still well?"

"Yes, but I haven't heard a more tragic love story for quite some time," Sinjen said, and finished his current glass.

He'd just started on the next when Harry walked in. "We need to go. Marlais just arrived in town. You'd best get yourself a cab, too, and get out. We'll keep him busy, but it goes without saying, you never spoke to either of us."

Sinjen and Sergiu downed their drinks in unison and the vampires left through the front door. The hunter paid and left through the back. The neighbouring table helped themselves to the toast, whiskey, ice and whelks that they had left, not even bothering to look embarrassed about it.

Harry and Sinjen kept an eye on Marlais for a little while, but he did not look for them. He went to a rather fine establishment that Harry assured him was a top-tier gentleman's club. Sinjen fed again, on a pretty beachgoer, then Harry suggested that they go back to Carol's. "It'll have to be hers; I'm known to be too sad to go to the nice one."

"That's not the nice one," Sinjen objected. "Oh. Did your girl die?"

"Oh yes; luckily I was there to hold her hand. Very sad, but I popped in for a few free drinks after it happened. The Madam was very sympathetic. She offered me some compatible replacements, but none really took my fancy." He sounded almost upset.

"How do you choose them?" Sinjen asked, as they were shown to a secluded table. It wasn't a private room, but a slightly screened booth. Harry asked for absinthe, insisting he had to drown his sorrows. The drink wasn't exactly popular but, as far as vampires were concerned, it got the job done.

Sinjen had the better view of the establishment, and could see that it too had been undergoing improvements. He hoped this was due to Carol and not Miriam. Carol did look content, and was flirting with a wealthy older man. Her manner was quite different when she was working. He'd have pointed it out to Harry, but he was considered to be one of the vampires who needed to constantly have victims, if only one at a time.

Sinjen insisted, to the few women who bothered them, that Harry was too sad tonight and they wanted privacy.

"Sinjen, I'll pull through," Harry complained.

"Go on, what do you look for? Tell me, as someone who doesn't fixate on a particular type."

He sighed. "Oh, you know. Just something in the eyes. An innocence, gentleness of spirit, I don't know. A trusting sweetness, or perhaps a little desperation."

"So, Carlotta, basically. When she was mine," Sinjen said coldly.

"Alright, sure, that type. I did turn her on purpose, you know," Harry said. He was reading the absinthe label and trying not to attract Sinjen's attention, even though they were the only two in this corner.

"What about the others?"

"Oh, sure. Some of them. I don't know. I wouldn't fixate on someone I couldn't bear to look at for an eternity, would I? My dear girls are beautiful, nobody would deny that."

"I suppose that's true. You look a bit of a fool trying to hide behind that bottle. You know I'm not angry with you, don't you?" Sinjen sighed.

"But that face you make is just awfu—"

"Shush," Sinjen insisted.

"You just said you weren't angry," Harry complained.

"Not that. It's our rogue again. Oh, but he's all dressed up tonight. I wonder if he's hunting." Sinjen whistled and waved him over. He did come to their table, but when he saw what they were drinking he went back to the bar and ordered finger sandwiches.

"Great, so now I'm having a ruddy tea party with two blokes," Harry complained when he'd been told.

"Don't mind him, Victor. He's grieving," Sinjen said sarcastically. Bickerstaff nodded and poured them each another drink. Sinjen went on, "There's going to be a death match tomorrow. Be our boy Alexander against the hunters. Or that's my guess, I'm not sure what will happen, actually."

"Death match sounds about right. That family loves a brawl. Are you two going to watch it?" Victor asked, sounding thrilled.

Harry and Sinjen exchanged a look. "I will," Sinjen answered, so Harry agreed too. "It's up on the headland."

"That sounds fantastic, we should have a great view," Victor said, grinning from ear to ear.

Harry started to laugh. "Ah, you haven't changed one bit. Mad bastard."

Victor and Harry began to get along quite well, so Sinjen arranged for some girls to go over to them before heading out. He wanted to get back to Miriam.

He spirited most of the way, but Marlais and Sora met him. He bowed low. "Where are you going on your own?" Marlais asked in an amused tone.

"One of my houses. I thought I might stay out tonight. Is that alright?"

Marlais laughed. "I'm not your mother, am I? Harry's meant to be watching you."

Sinjen frowned. "His latest girl died tonight, so I think he's drinking, or whatever he does afterwards. Do you want me to bring Sora with me?"

"Oh, nonsense," Marlais said with a smile. "You must come with us tonight. You like dancing, don't you?"

"I hate dancing, but I do like both of you."

Marlais looked back at him, over his shoulder. "I can't abide a wallflower. Go and play," he said and, taking Sora's arm, spirited them both away.

Sinjen took a deep breath and thought for a while. If he was being watched then he might put whoever he visited at risk, but he might also just be being paranoid. Marlais did like to play games. He could go and sulk at Eliza's place, maybe.

Mister Wright

Chapter 21

When Miriam had eaten, she felt quite a bit better, and asked Richard if she could smoke by the fire or if she should go outside.

He smiled. "If I told you the things Sinjen had done here, you wouldn't need to ask. Smoke away."

She took one of the remaining cigarettes Sinjen had left out for them last time, as Richard hadn't moved them from the mantelpiece. He lit it for her with a match. She asked him if he'd smoke with her. He agreed, without thinking anything of it. They sat down in armchairs, across from each other. It was a quiet night and very late; both were lost in their own thoughts.

"What's on your mind?" Richard asked after a while.

"Have you ever seen him kill someone?" Miriam asked.

"Yes, kind of."

"Kind of?" she said, irritated.

"If his mistress was around, then I've seen him kill. Dozens of people, and he does it just for her amusement. She's dangerous, but I know that he hates her, and I know he hates what he does for her. I was his primary servant for a while in my youth. He replaces us quite regularly, but his life was much worse when I was very young, compared to when I left. So, I suppose his approach has been working. I saw him, the things he suffered, his injuries, the things he did and the way it hurt him.

It's funny you ask that. I was wondering why I have always been able to speak freely about him. In fact, though I made a pact with him. After he bought me, and I'd been trained up a little, I'm not sure I was ever under any real restrictions. I don't know why. Do they only trick people into thinking they are thralls?"

Miriam raised an eyebrow. They'd finished their first cigarette. Though she was slightly lightheaded, she asked him to bring more wine and said she'd be back in a moment.

She went to the neighbouring house. Though the hour was unreasonable, the couple who lived there turned out to be very helpful when they heard her request.

"Excuse me, but do you by any chance have a cross or crucifix I might borrow? It's... I know it's strange, but it's a little bit important to me right now. I can bring it back tomorrow morning."

The old man raised his eyebrows, but the old lady nodded and pressed her necklace into Miriam's hands without a word.

"I don't know what it means to you, miss, but I hope it's useful," the old man said, as they went inside.

Miriam felt a little more moved than she'd expected to, and brought it back to Richard, who was refilling their glasses.

She showed him what she had acquired and asked him to put out his hand. The cross left no mark. She explained about the vampire hunters, and that Ardelean had done the same to her.

He ran his fingers through his hair. "Then I wonder why I'm not a thrall. I did as I was told. Does that mean that I might have left at any time?" Miriam shrugged. He took her arm and they sat together by the window sharing their smoke and sipping their wine. "Maybe I didn't want to leave him."

"Were you... close?" she asked, thinking of Jack. He was puzzled by the question. "His latest thrall, Jack, is rather fond of men, more so than women, I think."

Richard raised his eyebrows. "No, I'm not that way. I did ask him once, actually, why he never... I mean I didn't want to, or anything, but he's quite a flirt. You might have noticed. We never, I mean, he never even tried anything with me, and it seemed a bit odd. So I did ask him once. Is that foolish? I guess I was wondering if there was something wrong with me."

Miriam was laughing quietly to herself. Somehow, he hadn't noticed that she was leaning against him until he felt her body shaking at his side. He put his arm around her and she touched his hand. Her fingers were very cold, in spite of the warmth of the room. He recoiled slightly when he felt the chill of them, but she only murmured, "Cold hands, warm heart."

He held her, in case she was really cold but didn't want to admit it. "What did he say?" she asked.

"Oh, right. He said I was practically his own child, and he wouldn't dream of it."

"Then how old were you when he— he *bought* you?" Miriam asked. He'd said it, but it hadn't quite registered.

"Well, essentially, he compensated a mill for the value of my labour, and they let me leave with him. I was barely there for a week. I had a parent, by the way. She was just too drunk to care, I suppose. I don't think anyone ever looked for me after I left with him. I don't remember too well, but I think, Mother got herself out of the workhouse by marrying and just didn't bother coming back for me. I don't know if they knew each other, or if he was just recruiting."

Miriam interlaced her fingers with his and he did feel her hands finally start to warm up. "Then is it possible that you were not the correct age to form a contract? Is there an age?" she asked.

"Sinjen didn't do it until I was thirteen. So perhaps he was waiting until then. Should I ask him?"

"Would he make you a thrall if you did?"

Richard didn't seem sure, but Miriam was getting tired. As they had finished their wine, he showed her to her room.

He brought her up a washbasin and a hot water bottle as she was getting undressed.

She dipped behind the door when he came in, and he apologised, though she was very glad of both, especially as her feet and hands were cold from washing. It was colder upstairs than downstairs, even if the blankets were warm and thick. Sinjen had complained about the size of her bed before, and now she was wondering if he'd had a point.

After a while, though, it wasn't Sinjen who was on her mind but Richard. Sinjen was rather difficult. Though he was considerate and treated her well, Richard just felt...

She sighed. There was a candle next to her bed; she hadn't blown it out yet, so she inspected the room a little. In the wardrobe was a blue dressing gown. She put it on and went to find him.

Richard was reading the newspaper and waiting for Sinjen. It was long past midnight. He looked up at her and she froze on the steps.

"Miss Miriam?" he asked, a note of concern in his voice.

"There's a spider in my room?" she suggested, very shyly.

He laughed. "Alright, I'll save you." When they were in her room, she confessed that there wasn't actually a spider, but that she'd missed him. He looked a little shocked and she couldn't meet his eye.

She wasn't a virgin. Jack had been quite spirited at one point, and she really had thought they would marry before she discovered his other tendencies. It was only that she'd found herself unable, afterwards, to shake the feeling that she might have caused his inclinations. Or else, to give up the idea, she attracted a certain kind of man. Just at this moment, her courage was faltering, her hands trembling.

Richard took her hands and kissed her forehead, then took off his jacket and shoes. She let him take the dressing gown off her and hang it up. After a moment he decided to remove his vest, guided her back into bed and held her.

She rested her head on his arm and they clasped their hands together. Miriam leant her head against his chest. He drew her closer still, and kissed her forehead again.

"You know," she whispered, "If you wanted to do more..."

He kissed her on the lips, but refused. "I'll stay with you the whole night, if you want me to. We had too much wine, though, I think."

She nodded, and put her arm around him.

Sinjen arrived home to find the fire lower than usual and threw a few coals onto it. Downstairs was tidy, but he started to feel uneasy.

Sora had been here before, as had Harry. There wasn't much of a guarantee that the house was safe. He hadn't had it blessed for a while, either. He puzzled over a cross on the table, and stared at it for long enough that he started to get a bit of a headache. He knew Richard and Miriam didn't have one.

He wandered upstairs and checked Richard's room, which was empty. He opened the door to the guest room and found the two asleep in a sweet embrace. Miriam's hand looked like it might get cold, so he lifted the blankets over it.

She was a heavy sleeper, but Richard's eyes snapped open at once. He turned to look at Sinjen, a nervous twitch of his lips betraying his fear. Sinjen knelt and stroked Richard's hair. He let out a short, silent laugh, nothing more than a breath really, when he sensed how hard the man's heart was pounding in his chest. It did begin to slow when Sinjen smiled.

"I'm sorry," he whispered. "Nothing happened, I promise, but I think I like her."

The sinking feeling in his stomach hit Sinjen hard, and he swallowed before he whispered in return, "I'm not even insulted. If it's not me, then my son is a fair choice." His lip quivered very slightly, and he went downstairs so he wouldn't disturb them more.

He lay on the sofa, smoking and thinking that the night had been a disaster. His fledgling would die. The hunter's heart and Viola's would be breaking. Harry's girl had died, and he'd barely even spared her a glance. Victor and Harry would have a show to enjoy. The ring was long gone, too, so he wouldn't gain anything by it, and he'd really hoped to win favour with Petri.

There was a reasonable chance that the Ancient was getting irritated, and he might have to get himself thrown back into jail to take care of that. Eliza wasn't even *at* Moonlight, and therefore had no chance of being killed in one of the Ancient's moods.

Which meant she would come back, and he'd have to see her again. He'd probably have to get rid of Harry. That last just seemed sensible. He took a deep and shuddering breath. Oh, and Miriam had left him for his dear servant, which was the cherry on top.

Why had it hurt so much? Had he really liked her? He sat up and went to the garden to smoke in the fresh air. It was close to sunrise.

What could he do about most of his troubles? A few might have solutions, but he'd have to pick his battles. He lay down on Richard's neat gravel path, lost in thought, until one of the cockerels crowed and scared the life out of him. He hadn't stood up before the garden door opened, and Miriam came out in his dressing gown. Richard followed her with a lantern. He forgot, sometimes, that humans couldn't see that well in the dark.

"Sir, it's starting to get light. Can you mope somewhere safer?" Richard suggested.

"I'm an old man, I'll mope where I please," he huffed.

Miriam laughed. "So this is what you're like when you act your age."

Sinjen sat up, and followed them inside.

"Where will you sleep, sir?" Richard asked.

"There's no point being on your best behaviour, Richard. Not after taking my woman to bed." He heard them both gasp. "Why was there a cross on the table, by the way?"

"Don't worry about it," Richard said. "Miriam just felt like testing one on a thrall. Is it supposed to sting?"

"No. They say a prayer when they test thralls, or nothing happens, but we don't bring holy objects into the house. Are you alright?"

"I am."

"Show me," Sinjen insisted, and Richard held out his hand. Sinjen froze, then took Richard's face and looked into his eyes. He and Miriam were both terrified. "I see. That explains it all, doesn't it? Richard, you should have been... You knew what you did would hurt me. Didn't you?" The man's eyes widened further.

Sinjen kissed him on the lips, not affectionately, but like he'd just realised something wonderful. Then he released him, and Richard took a step back with a hand poised over his mouth. He cast a helpless glance at Miriam, who was stunned.

"What is it?" she asked, afraid of the answer.

"All this time, Richard, you've actually been genuinely loyal to me?" He started to pace around the room. He couldn't even keep his hands still; it was like they were acting out his thought processes. "Oh, I see. Oh, dear, that's rather sad. Do you recall, Richard, when you were, oh, eleven, I suppose, and you confronted me about your age? You said you were actually twelve, but that the mill had lied on your papers and said you were a year younger, so that they could keep you in their service, at a child's wage, for an extra year?"

"Yes, sir. You were amused and said you already knew. You said I was brave."

"Well, I thought I did know, because I'd checked with the workhouse you'd come from originally. They told me that your mother had been very specific about your age, and her own, but when they followed up, they found that her age was off by two years. I think that she must have lied about both of your ages. They did say that she was rather vain, or perhaps she genuinely did not remember. Dear, dear, I guess I was overfeeding you. I thought you were so small because you'd been so neglected. Well. You grew up well, in the end."

Sinjen really did seem happier, though the other two were still bemused.

"There is a bedroom prepared for you, sir," Richard said, after a pause.

"Stop calling me sir!" Sinjen snapped, making him jump. "If I wasn't poison, I'd adopt you. As it is, it can't even be official, but you call me Sinjen now."

"Yes... Sinjen," he said, haltingly, as he followed Sinjen up the stairs. Miriam trailed after them both.

"Miriam, you have to marry him. I insist."

Miriam let out a strange kind of choking sound, but could not follow it up with her usual dialogue. Richard turned and grinned at her. She hadn't noticed until then how many of Sinjen's mannerisms he'd picked up.

"Then, I'll have a son *and* a daughter, and I'll be very happy," he said, forgetting about the time he'd put his hand up her dress, though Miriam recalled it very keenly at that moment and blushed. "Richard, you might as well have this house too, but I will need you to let me in. That's not a condition, but I'll want to visit my *many* adorable grandchildren."

"Um. Sinjen, aren't you getting a bit ahead of yourself?" Miriam suggested.

"Nonsense, listen to your elder. Goodnight," he said, and pushed them both gently out of his room before shutting the door.

Miriam and Richard were left in the corridor. Miriam turned to him.

Richard cleared his throat. "He has these... funny moods. Sometimes."

"Yes. I think he does a bit," she admitted. They went back to bed, but this time in different rooms.

Parsley

Chapter 22

A t nightfall Sinjen woke, feeling rather happy, and put on a fresh suit. This one was brown, with a long frock coat and a light-coloured scarf. As it was winter, he also put on boots and gloves, and thought that might be reasonable. He'd misplaced his hat, possibly at the brothel.

Miriam arrived at the cottage by the time he was done. "I'm sorry if I'm late. I had so much work to do today."

Richard gave her a warm smile over his dusting.

"You're really planning to come to this?" Sinjen asked.

"Viola will be going and... I think, perhaps another woman should be with her," Miriam said, not quite meeting his eye. "She won't be used to anything like this either, she just wants to be there. I said I'd meet her at the Abbey. I don't want to impose on their last moments... She's with her son, too."

"It's not happening for hours yet. Two in the morning, so rest if you need to," Sinjen said, looking between Miriam and Richard. "I'd better go and check on Jack. For all I know he's already a quivering mess."

"He was very well when I saw him today," Richard contributed. "Actually, I think he's well-suited to that kind of work. Though he's not great at folding clothes."

"I can probably live with that," Sinjen conceded. "I'm going to borrow your horse."

"It's your horse, Si— Sinjen."

"Hah, you forgot what I said, didn't you? I'll have the paperwork sorted out too. Actually, you do that for me. You know my solicitor. Have him come here on Monday with the relevant papers. I will continue to make use of this house as I please, I'd like you to allow that."

"I suppose I can't argue, but I don't want other vampires here." Richard adjusted his sleeve, expression uncertain. The house wasn't huge, but it was pretty, and he was very fond of it. Sinjen had paid him enough over the years that he could be considered reasonably wealthy, but he'd never seriously considered getting married. It just didn't seem like something thralls did until they retired. He was still adjusting to the idea that he'd never been one. He snuck a shy glance at Miriam. It was probably best she never found out how much he'd lost cock-fighting and dog-racing over the years.

Sinjen grinned at him, guessing something of his thoughts. Miriam was quite happy to stay. She had been looking up at the door to the guest bedroom, and had endured a lot of late nights in the last few days. He kissed her on the cheek and went out.

Sinjen arrived at Eliza's and gave the horse over to her stablehand. The groom particularly liked this horse, and could be trusted bring him back later, if needed.

Sinjen found Jack in one of the bedrooms. He was being grilled by an amused-sounding Sora. "So, is your hair naturally red?" she asked, using her sweeter voice. Jack assured her it was. "Mine's out of a bottle, but don't tell anyone. I figure if I do it for long enough, people will forget it was ever any other colour."

Sinjen knocked politely and entered. He paused for a second, seeing Jack's expression. He was being leant on heavily by Sora, and was having some difficulty processing his feelings about it.

"Hey," Sinjen said by way of greeting, "I hope you're both having a good evening. May I retrieve my thrall?"

When they were back in his room, Jack asked, "Excuse me, Sinjen. I haven't been told if I can—"

"Yes, you can sleep with the vampiresses. I'd avoid the staff, and make your own fun with thralls, or whatever, during the day. Most of the vampiresses are alright, except for Lady Eliza and Lady Tansy, who you should avoid even seeing in the former case, and be very cautious of in the latter. I'm sure Lady Carlotta can tell you more.

I'm sure you would never, but just so you know, any interference with a vampire child is punishable by death, and Margaret usually does that before anyone else even hears about it. I'll let you know when someone especially dangerous shows up. Always beware of Lord Marlais, or anyone high-ranking."

"I assure you, I'd never even thought—"

"I know. I'm just telling you how it is. In general, it's better to avoid the male vampires too, unless you know them by reputation. You wouldn't think they'd be the more difficult, but they can be possessive, obsessive, sexually strange, or any combination thereof. It's not that the women can't be any of those things, it's just that they're... they're usually easier to deal with if there is a problem. With the exception of a few, including Lady Tansy, or so it is according to rumour. I did hear she has a particular fascination with redheads, which is why I'm warning you."

"Um, if I'd already...?" Jack asked, nervously.

"With Lady Tansy?"

"Lady Carlotta..."

"Oh, don't worry about it. She's fine, just a bit prone to biting." Sinjen sighed. He went to the doorway and said loudly in the direction of Carlotta's room, "That woman has the nerve to call me a ride, though. When she's no better." Hearing her laughter, he returned to Jack. "How are you settling in?"

Jack threw himself down on one of the armchairs and beamed at him. "It's pretty nice, guv."

"Oh, good. You aren't my usual type, but I'm hoping you'll turn out to be useful." Sinjen lay back on his bed. "You know, Miriam's already gone off me."

Jack laughed. "Yeah, she does that. Did to me, anyway, but we weren't really that well suited."

"How did you even meet her?"

"In the library." Sinjen sat up and considered him. "What? I can read, at least a little. But I was looking at maps; my friend has a boat and—"

"You were smuggling?" Sinjen asked.

"Just a few things for Carol. Well, not for her, but she had a few patrons requesting unusual drinks and in the end it was the easiest thing. It was quite fun."

"You got caught?"

"No, Carol's made a few connections, and she doesn't really think it'll be a problem if they keep their operation small. She says it all gets taxed her end anyway, and with the up-charge it amounts to the same as import would have been," Jack elaborated.

"So she really is enterprising? I knew I liked her."

They talked for a long time, until Sinjen checked his pocket watch and excused himself.

Lord Marlais was here again, he saw him in the hallway, but his expression was serious. He and Eliza's residences were practically within spiriting distance, so they freely came and went from one estate to the other. Their properties were large enough that they didn't have to see each other if they didn't want to.

"No new love interests yet?" Sinjen hazarded.

This caused Marlais to look more unhappy. "I hate being single. I know it's a feeble thing for a man to say, especially to a confirmed old bachelor like yourself, but it makes me absolutely miserable."

Sinjen patted him on the shoulder, and ignored the sting of his comment. "What's your type?"

He let out a long sigh. "This time, I think a timid girl. Something pretty, but not too beautiful, with a round face and big eyes. Young and still eager to please. Something like that."

Sinjen smiled and nodded. Marlais chose his wives like other men might choose a style of suit, or something off a wine menu. The last one, he'd insisted, must have frizzy long hair, be tall, but not too tall, with long limbs and the kind of smile that took up most of her face. A smile that was hard to take your eyes off.

"By a small error of Eliza's, I think there might be a girl like that here," Sinjen suggested. "I'm afraid you might have a job nursing her back to health after all she's been through, and she'll know what you are."

"Oh, but Sinjen, that's ideal! That's just what I want. I want to see one come out of her shell, and have some hope for the future. The last one was all breaking down. This one with careful rebuilding first. Oh, I do love when I get to be nurturing."

The absolute evil delight in his voice was not betrayed, even slightly, by his face, which had retained the entirety of its cheerful and almost puppy-like excitement. Marlais was much scarier when he got bored of his mask. Sinjen by now knew him well enough that he hardly bothered with it.

Sinjen bowed and brought the little hairdresser to his room. She was petrified, and Marlais was entirely taken with her. She was tiny, angelic, and would be beautiful if her hair wasn't so fine and thin. Most likely, she had lost a great deal to stress.

Sinjen put on a little act for them. It really wasn't worth Marlais being bored and keeping his attention on him instead. He had her little frame in his arms and could feel her helpless desperation to flee the room. "This one, Lord Marlais? Would she please you for tonight? Eliza was going to have killed her by now, but she's been quite fun already. Would you like to see the damage?" he asked, motioning as if he would lift her skirt. The girl cried out in panic and Marlais let her flee into his arms.

"Sinjen! I can see she's been through quite enough already, the little dear." The girl's head was pressed against his chest, and so he didn't bother concealing his expression. He beheld Sinjen with naked glee, his eyes sparkling.

He took a breath and became the picture of genuine concern. "My goodness, what happened to her hands?" He took one and examined it. The girl would know who he was. Yet, much as a drowning man might clutch at a straw, she seized every hope he offered when he affected compassion.

She looked helplessly between Sinjen and Marlais, but he held her hand steady, and appeared so calm and concerned that she answered with a trembling voice, "Lady Eliza was not happy with my work, I accidentally pulled her hair."

Sinjen smiled and went to leave, but Marlais shook his head very slightly. "Tell me what she did, dear," he asked. "Sinjen, pour a brandy for her nerves. Use the one with the silver lid."

Sinjen went over to the table and poured the drink. As the only bottle with a silver lid was laudanum, he added enough of that to knock her out.

"What's your name, pet? Don't be frightened. You're quite safe," Sinjen heard, as he stirred the brandy and added some apple to garnish.

"I'm Elsie." He asked again what Eliza had done. "She burnt me, Lord Marlais. Then made me hold my hands still while she used some needles."

Marlais sighed, sounding sympathetic, but Sinjen knew he was only disappointed by the lack of detail.

He gave her the drink and spoke to her while the girl lost consciousness. Sinjen tried to leave a second time, but Marlais again shook his head. Sinjen tried to suppress his rising fear.

He watched Marlais lift the girl's dress and examine her other injuries. "You aren't going to hurt her, are you?" he asked, backing closer to the door. Marlais looked up with a grin, then walked towards Sinjen. "No, I won't hurt her, but I *will* hurt you."

Sinjen escaped the room after about an hour, at about the time the girl woke, and retreated to his room. Jack was waiting for him there; he must have been behind the door.

Jack's hands were shaking and he'd paled considerably. "What happened? I heard your screams, but Lady Carlotta told me to stay away from the door. She made me wait here."

Sinjen laughed, even though tears fell from his eyes. He wiped them away, cleaned himself up, and dressed again. "It was my fault. I should have left through a window instead of the bloody hallway." He took a breath, still trembling. "He'd have found me sooner or later, though. He hasn't been horrible enough to me in a while."

Jack held him, but he was at risk of being late. "Comfort me later. I have to go."

"But Sinjen—"

"You'll get used to it after a while. Just keep yourself safe," he said and spirited to his horse.

They did all get used to it, but he tried not to think about how that made him feel. If Carlotta hadn't stopped Jack from opening Marlais' door, he would be dead already. He stroked Parsley's mane and hoped his feelings wouldn't upset the creature. He really did like this horse because, as well as being good-natured, he didn't mind being spirited when he was in a hurry.

He made it to his cottage before he was nearly wiped out by Harry in what must be his spare car. His horse reared and Sinjen made a mental note to smack Harry when he caught up to him.

Richard came out to soothe the animal while Sinjen spirited with Miriam towards town. He spotted a pair of drunks halfway and left Miriam on a roof while he fed from them. "They weren't harmed," he explained, "but I got hurt again, and I'm not facing hunters without fresh blood."

She only complained about being left on the roof, so Sinjen kissed her cheek.

Miriam spotted Alexander, Viola and her son walking towards the Abbey, so Sinjen brought her down to them. She followed them at a distance, but it was better that she arrived with Viola than with him.

The hunters were already waiting on the headland. Sinjen joined Harry on the wall of Whitby Abbey, where they had a good view of the scene. The ruin of an impressive monument, the holy site was older than England itself, but there could be few enough people who understood its significance. He wasn't entirely certain whether the Abbey had ever been totally finished. It had been an ambitious project, long after the Synod of Whitby.

In a few moments, they were joined by Bickerstaff. He was in his disguise again. The three stood side by side and watched Alexander and the others walk up to his family.

There were three hunters there already. Alexander the fourth was waiting with his wife and Ardelean. All were armed.

Sinjen had to admit that Mrs. Varkov looked as dramatic and fierce as he'd expected. She was an impressively built woman, but had a narrow waist. She was wearing a dress with cape sleeves, and an expensive hat.

It would take a second look to see that her arm wasn't in the right one. It only became obvious when the wind blew that sleeve against her side. She, like the others, carried a weapon, and wore at least one more pistol that Sinjen could see. He noted it was an older design, but custom-made.

The hunters looked up at their vampire audience, but seemed less concerned after Ardelean pointed at each of them in turn and explained what he knew about them. All had reacted when Bickerstaff first appeared, but then began to laugh.

"Ah. They know I'm only here to watch the fight," Victor chuckled.

Alexander the fifth ran towards them, but paused for a moment before he got too close. They spoke at a distance, before his mother went to hold him, and his father embraced him too.

Ardelean also hugged him, then unscrewed a bottle of vodka. He poured them each a glass, including the boy, Viola and Miriam. Viola didn't seem to want hers, and the group laughed when Miriam downed it for her. Harry nudged Sinjen and said he was a bad influence.

Death Match

Chapter 23

M iriam held Viola's arm, and had to steady her more than once as events proceeded. After their toast, there was a small argument about who would fight Alexander. His father volunteered, but Ardelean wouldn't allow him to. Instead, it was decided that Ardelean would fight.

Miriam watched the vampires. This was partly to distract herself as the men embraced, said their last goodbyes and had their final toast as brothers.

The vampires were standing in a row; all were of a similar height, though Sinjen was the shortest. He was standing elegantly and smoking again, watching events with cold dispassion.

Harry seemed more impatient, and was the largest of the three men, if you ignored Bickerstaff's heavy cloak. Sinjen had told her that it was slightly padded. She watched Harry stretch his arms and look at the sky for a moment. His figure was rather wonderful.

Bickerstaff was standing boldly, like a soldier. When the wind blew his cloak against him, his figure resembled Ardelean's or Alexander's. Very strong and noble. He must have died quite young. He had the air of someone at the peak of their strength, and who knew it.

Viola weakened in her arms again, watching Alexander say his last words to his son. He apologised that he had never known him before he died, and for losing his battle with Bickerstaff. He told the boy to obey his grandfather and mother. To grow up strong. He said that, if nothing else, he could be an example to him of how to face death bravely.

The boy clung to his father for a time. When he was ready, Alexander pulled away and called to Ardelean, "Sergiu, I won't go easy on you. If you lose, I might well leave and make my own way. I have options."

Ardelean grinned, and they took their positions. Alexander struck first, but Sergiu severed his fingers with his sword.

Miriam gasped. She and Viola held one another. She was supporting them both at this point, but Viola wouldn't look away. Alexander spirited behind Sergiu in an instant and slashed his back, but even that visibly harmed him. When he pulled his hand away it was burnt red. Ardelean was able both to strike and block, to a degree, with the cane sheath. At one point he struck Alexander across the face with the cane, and the silver tip left hardly more injury than the rest of it.

His mother gasped, and turned to her husband, "He's blooded, we were too late," she whispered.

Alexander senior took her hand, his expression watchful and hard.

"They have to eat when they are young. It was always likely," he replied.

Miriam shuddered. She'd suspected already. He'd spent so long looking for Viola that those women who looked like her could have been too hard to resist.

She glanced at Sinjen again. He was so still that he might have been a statue. Harry was much more focused now and Bickerstaff had knelt down, almost like a gargoyle, to get a better view.

The fight was savage. Alexander's strikes were wild and desperate, but he was a trained fighter. His movements were so fast that Miriam could hardly follow them with her eyes. He landed a punch with his injured hand, which was so hard Ardelean was pushed back several feet, though he did not fall. Ardelean was winning, his strikes precise and strategic. He left several deep cuts, one severing a tendon in Alexander's arm and causing the injured arm to become unusable. Another pierced a lung, from the sound of it, but it did not slow him down for long.

After a few moments, Alexander was able to breathe normally again, though blood fell from his lips each time he exhaled. She watched Ardelean, slashed from inner elbow to chest by the vampire, then they stopped moving. Alexander's head resting on the shoulder of his brother in arms. Ardelean had pierced his chest as he'd gone in for the strike.

She saw Alexander whisper some words, then his mouth opened, showing fangs. Ardelean twisted the blade, yanking it upwards, and Alexander collapsed. He was laid on the ground. Ardelean drew a knife and removed the vampire's heart, piercing it again with the sword to be certain.

Viola pressed her face into Miriam's shoulder, her eyes filled with tears, before she straightened up, went over to her son and held him. They waited as the hunters examined the body, wrapped it in a shroud and carried it to their carriage.

Miriam jumped as Sinjen materialised beside her. "Should we go?" he asked.

Little Alexander piped up, "Vampires aren't real. Are you trying to pretend to be one too?"

Sinjen considered him. "We are very real. How rude. I don't question your existence."

The child thought about this. "That doesn't prove anything."

"Very well." Sinjen knelt down. "Put that cross on my arm," he said, pulling his sleeve back a little.

The boy did, and saw the mark it left. "Show me your fangs," he demanded.

Sinjen obliged, pulling back his lip.

"Then, when I grow up, I'm supposed to kill you?"

"Well, yes, that's the general idea. Will you?"

"I suppose I'd be obliged to," the boy admitted, still processing events.

Sinjen shook his hand. "Well, then, I'm Sinjen Carlyle. I look forward to seeing you when you've grown up."

A shot rang out. Sinjen reached for Miriam and spirited them to the top of the Abbey, where Harry caught him. "Take us to Carol," he whispered, before he collapsed. Harry disappeared with him at once.

Miriam watched Alexander's grandmother take hold of the child and check he was unharmed. "Bickerstaff, would you mind putting me back down? I'll join the others later." He nodded and left, the moment he'd put her back on the headland.

"Mrs. Varkov?" she called, running towards the woman. She was shouting at Viola for letting a vampire get too close. Viola was unable to respond, as she was throwing up on the grass.

"My name is Sasha," the woman said coldly, and pointed her gun at Miriam. "Who are you, and why are you consorting with the undead?"

Ardelean shouted, running towards them both, his arm still dripping blood, "She's okay, Sasha! She's not a thrall."

Sasha was still fuming, and shouted at Viola again. Her grandson got angry and shouted something back.

"You can't shout at her!" Miriam insisted. "Can't you see she's been through quite enough in her... in her..."

The patriarch of the family had returned and put his hand on his wife's shoulder. Ardelean was helping Viola to her feet.

"Her what?" Alexander the fourth asked, his tone deadly serious.

"Her condition," Miriam finished. "That's why I came with her. I don't know why she insisted that she had to be here, but she did. I was worried, also, that she'd be afraid to tell you."

Viola did look rather terrified. The hunters only looked from one to another. Sasha apologised, and asked if it was really true.

"I think so," Viola said. "I don't know if it's... normal, but I've felt so very nauseous, and I have these dreams, and... I keep thinking of blood. Is it supposed to be like that?"

Sasha covered her mouth and turned away. Ardelean took Viola's hand and pressed it against the cross he wore; it left no mark at all.

"It might be..." Alexander said slowly. "We'll have to check our records. This isn't something that happens every day. Sergiu, don't come back with us. Get fixed up, then ride to Canterbury and speak to the Abbot about his library."

Ardelean nodded.

"Girl... I mean, Viola, I'm sorry for what happened before. I was wrong then, time only showed it more clearly. If... if you turn out to be correct, though, you can't imagine what a blessing it would be to our family. A dhampir... A real half-vampire would be..."

"Let's not put the carriage before the horses," Sasha sighed. "We will see what happens, but we have one grandson and he's blessing enough. Let's go. We can't let her stand in the wind all night."

Miriam watched them go: Viola escorted by Ardelean, and little Alexander holding the hands of both his grandparents.

Miriam turned and made the long walk down the hill. It was very cold, and she hurried down, worried about Sinjen. In a moment she had to stop and run to the beach, where she too was sick.

She went over to the steps and sat for a moment, wrapping her stole around herself while she recovered. In her case, it was only the excitement, but she envied Viola. To be blessed with two children, while she had none, and had so desperately wanted a family since she had lost her mother.

She covered her eyes and began to cry.

She was like that for many minutes before there was a tap on her shoulder. She was afraid it was a police officer, but it was only Bickerstaff. He handed her a handkerchief and sat on the step beside her. He didn't say anything, but let her collect herself.

"Sinjen's been telling me all about you," she said after a few more minutes. The wind was still strong down here, but at least the sea air was familiar, and she could hear the sounds of town.

"He doesn't know anything about me," Bickerstaff said, sounding a little bit sad. He was watching a family comb the beach, only daring to look over at Miriam once in a while, when she didn't look too distressed.

"I think I do," Miriam said, and turned to him. Victor backed away considerably. She laughed at his reaction but then burst into tears again.

Victor sighed and came closer to her again. "Could you stop that? I've never really known how to deal with distressed women."

"I'm doing my best, honestly. It's been a trying time. I wasn't really expecting any of this when Sinjen asked me about my book."

"Which book?" Victor asked, looking at her out of the corner of his eye.

"It was *Dracula*," she admitted. He laughed, and she did too.

"Harry sent me to fetch you. Sinjen should be alright, though, don't worry. Carol is just sending for a doctor who doesn't ask questions. You might be better off staying here for a bit and skipping the gore, to be perfectly honest."

"Is he hurt badly?" she asked.

"Yes, but when they get the bullet out, he should heal." She stood, and had to lean on him to steady herself. "Look, are you quite alright?"

"Yes. Only my foot has gone numb," she said. "As I should wait to feel it again, can I please look at your beard? I assume it's false. I don't think your hair is even black. Am I right?"

He sighed. "Take a look." She pulled a bit of his beard. It was convincing, but the edge came off after some tugging. "That does hurt, you know."

"I think you're a blond," Miriam accused, and he chuckled. "I think you were once from the Wolfsbane clan, and I think Harry might have turned you because he thought it would be funny, or something. He seems like someone who might do something like that. You just didn't stay dead afterwards, and I think, in a funny sort of way, he's been trying to protect you."

Bickerstaff's eyes widened but he said nothing.

"If I'm right," Miriam continued, "you should tell Sinjen and ask him for his advice. I think he's suspected something similar himself. He was rather puzzling over your costume. In fact, whatever the story is, you should tell him. He and Harry... if they aren't friends, seem to have some kind of arrangement between them."

"Let's see them. Hopefully the doctor has already treated the wound," Victor said, letting her take his arm as they climbed the stairs. She'd worn the pretty dress that Sinjen had bought for her again tonight. It wasn't that she was in any particular disguise, only she didn't think anyone she knew would see her dressed so differently and automatically think 'Miriam.' Her clothes weren't as sober and unremarkable as she was.

"Do you know you have blood on your dress?" Victor asked.

Miriam looked at the stain and sighed. "Alexander's fingers..." Bickerstaff patted her on the back and laughed. "Do you really like violence that much?" she asked.

"Not violence, per se, but a really good fight is a thrill. The Varkovs all know that. Alexander, too. They would all rather he had died that way than in his sleep. It was better."

"Is that why you fight them too?" she asked, concerned.

"What, me? No, I just think it's fun." He laughed.

A Little Abnormal

Chapter 24

Miriam entered the room to find Sinjen lying across a bed over several bloodsoaked towels. They were in the brothel's main building, but away from the guest areas.

She could not see his injury, as the doctor was bent over the wound. Sinjen was facing away from her. She heard him cry out, as the doctor pulled the bullet from his side and it again burnt his skin.

The doctor went to a dish of water and rinsed the bullet off, while Harry pressed a bandage over the wound.

"That's all we need, Doctor," Harry insisted. "We can take care of the rest."

The doctor turned the bullet over in his hand. It was a perfect ball of silver, with symbols all over it. "What manner of weapon was this?" he asked, and then shook his head. "No, never mind."

"Can I keep the bullet?" Sinjen asked, sounding a little childish.

The doctor chuckled. "Of course. I'll leave you some antiseptic, gauze and bandages. If you need anything further, then call me again." He was bent over, tiding his tools away. "I think it's unlikely that he'll live, unless you have your own skilled doctors. There was considerable internal damage."

Harry gestured Miriam over to keep pressure on the wound, and led the doctor outside. She heard him hypnotise the doctor into believing that what he had seen was the consequence of an illegal duel. Nothing of particular note, and not as severe as it had seemed. The doctor plodded away and Harry returned. "Sinjen, what do you fancy?"

"Not one of the unfortunate women, Harry. Not an employee either, they were attacked recently," Sinjen said, his teeth gritted with pain.

"Customer it is," Harry grinned, and went to find one.

Miriam offered Sinjen her wrist but he shook his head. "If I bite you, I'll go too far. It's a sweet offer, though."

Victor raised his eyebrows and took one of the seats at the end of the room, at a plain wooden table with two chairs. The room was tucked away, more basic than most of the others, but still reasonably sized. He imagined it might be for staff, or perhaps injuries like this. Looking around, he could see a poison cabinet and out of morbid curiosity took a look. It was well stocked, and contained a few abortive blends, but was innocent enough overall. Injury treatment, pain relief and medicines to induce vomiting. This was the sickroom, then; it even had its own little sink and mirror.

Victor held Miriam while Sinjen ate, so that she would not see, but to his surprise the man took little, then let the customer go. Harry had evidently considered this so normal for him that he'd brought two instead of one, and made both forget what had happened.

Sinjen sat up after a little while. Though he was still visibly injured, the wound was closing well. He didn't bother putting a shirt on and didn't seem the slightest bit concerned to be undressed in front of Miriam. Miriam pulled away from Victor and returned to her seat, also regarding Sinjen's nudity without particular interest or alarm. Though, with amusement, Victor noticed her eyes flit over his chest once or twice.

"Harry?" Miriam asked. "Would you mind going out for a little bit, I'd like to speak to these two?"

Harry cast an uncertain look at Victor, but nodded and went to get a drink. "Oh, I'll book us a private room here, Sinjen. I can't imagine you're in a hurry to return."

"Eliza…"

"No, she won't be back for two days yet. Don't fret." Harry strode out, then returned, a little sheepishly, to shut the door.

"You eat rather gently, Sinjen. It's a little abnormal," Victor said. "Do you always leave it to chance?"

"I've seen enough suffering," Sinjen sighed. "What am I being told? It's something awful, isn't it?"

Miriam laughed. "Are you disoriented?"

"Could I have a brandy? I think I'm only stunned by my own stupidity."

"To be fair, little Alexander was rather precocious," Miriam smiled.

"They don't raise stupid children in that family," Victor added, pouring Sinjen a brandy from the poison cabinet.

Sinjen drank some and coughed. "The hell is this?"

"Tincture of wild lettuce," Victor explained.

"Oh, good, that's perfect. Anything for a bit of a boost?"

He returned to the cabinet and picked up a bottle. Sinjen told him to ignore the question, and fished out one of his cigarettes instead.

Miriam cleared her throat loudly and cracked the window open, ignoring Sinjen's protests. He shut it himself and gave her a stern look. "I'm hurt. I might catch my death."

"Can vampires get sick?" she asked. Sinjen and Victor both laughed. "Oh, fine. Victor has something to confess."

"We don't really do confession, but I'll hear your sins, my son," Sinjen said with a grin.

"Thank you, Father," Victor said, sarcastically. "My real name is Alexander Varkov the second. As Miriam correctly guessed, I died at the hands of Harry Balcom, I suppose, a generation before the end of Daylight. I lose track, to be perfectly honest.

Like an idiot, I went after some of the vampires who had killed me and, though only Harry knew I'd died, they weren't impressed. I ended up with a bounty, but nobody else ever found out I'd turned, so it should be redundant at this point. Through a series of stupid errors, I ended up with a bounty from humans too, and so I produced rumours of my death. I had to kill a few Varkovs, so that they forgot me. Only my grandson suspects who I truly am, but he's shown... discretion."

"You're aware that your whole family is... they're at some risk of dying out?" Miriam asked. "Without Viola's son, they would have no heirs."

Victor sighed. "Very well, I'll leave them alone. At least for a few generations, but—" he grimaced "—I won't enjoy it."

Sinjen chuckled. He watched Victor go over to the basin and start to pull off his disguise. First the ugly whiskers, then the beard. He washed the dark dye from his hair, with moderate success, leaving his hair a reddish brown instead of pale blond. Finally, he removed his heavy coat and padding.

Sinjen whistled. "Well, what do you know? It's Alexander the fifth all over again."

Varkov laughed. "He did rather resemble me, didn't he? It does make me a little proud, the... hmm... the strength of our bloodline. Just a shame the littlest Alexander is darker, but it happens from time to time, I suppose. He has the look, and the brains, anyway."

"What will he do now, Sinjen?" Miriam asked. "Is there anything that can be done?"

"Of course. Go and fetch Harry, dear sweetheart."

Miriam gave him a funny look, but did as he asked.

"She still has blood on her dress. You ought to get her a new one," Varkov said.

"Look, if she'd accept my money, I'd give her anything she could wish, but that's neither here nor there. I'd like to ask you about a red ring. I'm quite interested in it."

Varkov pulled a gold necklace out of his shirt. A ring was hanging from it. "The Varkovs took it, and used it as an emblem of leadership. My son wore it for a time, and when I defeated him, I took it back. Why?"

"That item has a bounty of its own. It would be unwise for you to keep it," Sinjen explained.

Varkov passed it to him. "You want it?"

"Please. I do appreciate it." Sinjen smiled.

Harry returned just as Sinjen pocketed the ring. "I'm told I'm wanted?" he said, then paused, looking at the change in Varkov. "What now?" he asked, turning to Sinjen with suspicion.

"Might your little child pretend to be our fledgling?"

Harry frowned, then smiled. "Sure. I gave the name Vadim Volkov. Thought it was funny. We just want a story."

Sinjen grinned. "No story. Nobody ever found out about our rogue, so we don't need to explain him away. You killed a sailor, and he looks promising. I, for my part, had a run-in with Wolfsbane and killed Alexander the fifth. Can either of you see any problems with that?"

Harry thought for a while. "Besides the problem of his strength and knowledge, then no. It's usually easy enough to spot a fledgling by their doe eyes and, if tasted, their blood. Varkov, can you look more clueless and afraid?"

He shrugged and raised an eyebrow. "What if you tell them I was a boxer? Would they expect me to be so afraid then? It would explain my build."

Sinjen and Harry considered him with interest, then grinned at each other. "Yes, why not?" Harry laughed.

Miriam watched proceedings in silence. They seemed to have forgotten that she was there. Had she been neglected because she was only food to them all?

"I should change my dress," she said, attempting to sound feeble.

Sinjen looked at her with some sympathy. "My clothing has been quite ruined too. Let me take you home, and I'll order you something nice."

Harry scowled. "You're injured."

"You think I haven't been injured before? If anyone is used to it, I am," Sinjen hissed.

Miriam and Harry exchanged a concerned glance, then turned to him. "Sinjen, we care about you," Miriam pleaded.

"Then don't tell me I'm weak," he said, pulling himself up. "Miriam, it's meaningless to argue." He gripped her arm, more painfully than he had before, and brought her to the door of the tailor's shop.

The woman he'd bought the curtains from answered and, seeing Sinjen, ushered them in.

"Three nice dresses for the woman, sensible attire, though, and I need some clean clothes."

He'd only put his shirt on over his bloodstained trousers. The woman took in the holes in his shirt, and the blood-soaked cloth. She willingly ignored his pristine skin and healthy appearance, instead looking at Miriam's worry lines and exhausted expression, before turning back to him and nodding. "As you wish, Lord Carlyle."

Miriam glared at him as the tailor bustled away and woke her family.

"It's not my fault, dearest one. Humans set so much store by titles. I did myself once." He looked down, half sighed, half grimaced with disgust, and then added, "Be with me. I don't mind how it's arranged. When you tire of me, split from me, and I'll leave you more than you could wish. Even I can see how much your body cries out for a child. Take a surrogate, even my son, for that purpose. Only belong to me. The boy is young still, he will recover, but you..."

Miriam gasped, afraid of how she might respond. After a moment's turmoil, she ran from the shop and did not stop running until she got home.

Sinjen watched her go with some amusement. He shouldn't have said those things to her, he wasn't even sure why he had. Jealousy, perhaps. The tailor brought him out a clean shirt, but she had nothing else that was suitable, so he thanked her. It didn't matter that much, as he would spirit anyway, but there had been a lot of blood.

He stopped at the cottage and took his time cleaning up and dressing. Afterwards he found Richard in the garden. He was burning some dead wood, with his back to the door. Sinjen watched him for a time, walked over and put his arms around him. Richard jumped, then sighed and let Sinjen pull him close. His feet were still where they had been, but his back was against Sinjen's chest.

Miriam, after she had recovered from the shock of Sinjen's words, had also walked to the cottage. She heard voices from the garden, and so crept around the back. She froze when she could make out their words, and inched a little closer to see what was happening.

"Say you love me," Sinjen was saying. Richard didn't reply, but shook his head. Sinjen stroked the grey streak of hair above his ear. "You used to tell me all the time. Why not now?"

"I love you," Richard said, a little reluctantly.

"That's all I get?" Sinjen sounded offended. "You should give me kisses, and a cuddle."

"Oh, must I?" Richard sighed. There was a small scuffle. In the end, Miriam could see Sinjen on all fours above Richard, peppering his face with kisses. "We're in the garden. Someone will see."

"I don't care," Sinjen insisted, and continued to kiss him until Richard wrapped his arms around him. Miriam felt quite sick and headed back to town.

"Why are you like this?" Richard asked, holding Sinjen's head against his chest to keep him still.

"Demonstrative?" He laughed. "Because life is short, and I want the people I love to know I love them."

"When did I ever say I loved you?" Richard asked, pushing Sinjen away and getting to his feet.

"Ah, you used to say it all the time, when you were a boy. I'd tuck you into bed and you'd say, 'I love you, Mr. Carlyle,' and I'd pat you on the head. But I loved you too, you do know that?"

"Yes, I know," Richard said, letting him back into the house. "In the morning you'd leave a sweet or something on the bedside table. I do remember, now that you say it."

"Oh. Were you just manipulating sweets out of me?" Sinjen complained.

Richard looked away, a little sheepish. "Well, maybe a little bit."

Sinjen laughed. "But you had a good childhood? You felt loved enough?"

"I did." Richard hugged him properly. "Are you sleeping here tonight?"

"No, I'm expected home. I got shot tonight, actually. Nothing to fret about, but it's been a difficult night. I wanted to see you before I went back."

"Great, something else to keep me up at night."

Sinjen smiled. "You shouldn't worry about me so much. You're ageing before your time. You have your whole future ahead of you."

All Kinds of Monsters

Chapter 25

Miriam hadn't made it the whole way home before a car slowed to a halt beside her. Harry was in it. "Miss Green, what on earth are you doing wandering about alone at night? There could be all kinds of monsters about."

"I thought you were staying in town?" she asked.

"Well, I think I will. Except I was going to take a trip home and get a change of clothes and my toothbrush. Do you want to come with me?"

"Is it safe?" she asked, doubting very much that it could be.

"I'll look after you, and I'll drive slowly. Not that you should ever turn up unannounced. Do you like my car? Sinjen's just bought a new one for me, only I won't get it for a few months. Still, it should be the latest design."

He came around and opened the door for her. She got inside and looked the vehicle over. She'd never seen a nicer one, or many at all, and it was still very shiny and new. "It's lovely."

Harry smiled and drove, at a more reasonable pace, back to the house. He took Miriam's hand when they arrived and led her in. There were quite a number of thralls and vampires in the reception rooms, playing cards, drinking and watching a small, bawdy play.

Harry did not let go of her hand, even for a second, and took her upstairs. She stared when she passed Sinjen in the hall. He saw her, but his aspect was cold and he gave no sign that he'd recognised her. He only scowled and continued to stride toward his room.

"Don't worry," Harry whispered, "that's how he is at home."

He opened one of the doors and let her in, releasing her hand. "Carlotta, my darling, would you keep an eye on this little mite while I pack a bag?"

A captivating beauty with light auburn hair turned to her. She was feeding a cheerful blue budgie. Miriam felt Carlotta's eyes scan her body and clothing. She covered the worst of the bloodstains with her hand. Even though this was the fanciest dress she owned, she felt underdressed and scruffy, both generally and in front of the woman, who only smiled slightly at her embarrassment.

The door closed behind her and she saw that Harry was gone. Her heart started to race, but she tried not to show it.

"Are you Harry's latest girl?" Carlotta asked.

"Um, no. I'm just... I'm Sinjen's friend, actually."

"My word, did Sinjen bring you here?"

"No, Harry did. I don't think he had any particular reason, I just passed him in the street," Miriam replied.

"Oh, well, that's alright then. You shouldn't hang around, but come here, I can't let you leave in that dress. You look a sight." Her voice was pretty and husky, her expression much more gentle and serene than Miriam would have expected. Carlotta stood and walked towards her wardrobe. Her figure and motions, even her expression and the way her hair moved, seemed unbearably pretty and elegant.

"You're the one Harry is in love with?" Miriam asked, without meaning to speak. Carlotta looked back over her shoulder at her and smiled coquettishly. "And even Sinjen?"

Carlotta laughed. "Did he say that?"

"Um, no. But, well, they both speak well of you," she said, a small blush rising to her cheeks.

Carlotta smiled more warmly and pulled a few items out of her wardrobe. "This is last season, so you can keep it, alright? It should fit you well enough. You had better have an under-layer too, because it's a little thin for the weather. We don't feel the cold, you see."

Miriam nodded and let Carlotta help her dress. She'd picked out a blue skirt, a delicate white blouse, an undershirt and a blue ribbon. The skirt had an oversized bow down the back.

Carlotta wrapped the rest of Miriam's clothes in brown paper, except for her stole, which she would need, and removed Miriam's hat. She tidied her hair, which had already faced the wind on the headland, and fastened it with the ribbon. Miriam looked more like herself, and yet so drastically different that she couldn't take her eyes off the mirror. She let Carlotta dab a little pink powder on her cheeks and mist her with something rose scented. She'd done it all so efficiently that when Harry returned, he looked at Miriam twice before he recognised her.

"Bloody hell, Carlotta. What witchcraft is this?" he exclaimed.

"Oh. She was already pretty, dear Henry. Couldn't you tell?" she drawled, and returned to her magazines.

Harry grinned and took Miriam's hand again. He knocked on Sinjen's door and was let in by Jack. Miriam did a double take when she saw him. Jack looked dashing, with a bit of a roguish air to him. She knew he'd never had the money to spend on luxurious clothing before, but he must have been thinking about it. He'd chosen an outfit that made the most of his figure. It wasn't a standard servant's uniform, but something more colourful and dapper. Sinjen was writing a letter and turned to them, his expression just as severe as before.

However, when he saw Miriam, he couldn't help smiling. "What's all this?"

"I left Miriam with Carlotta for a couple of minutes. I thought you'd like to see," Harry explained.

"My Miriam?" Jack laughed. "Goodness, it *is* her. Aren't you pretty?"

Miriam blushed and couldn't look at either of them, instead looking at Harry and then at the door. Harry took the hint. "I'm just taking her home. I found her wandering about near your cottage, Sinjen. You didn't let her walk home alone in the middle of the night, did you?"

Sinjen grew serious again. "No. Oh, Miriam... we may have had another misunderstanding."

"Funny how it's the same misunderstanding every time, isn't it?" she snapped, and took Harry's arm. He shrugged at Sinjen and walked her to the car. Harry asked her what was wrong, but she wouldn't answer.

When they returned to Whitby, Harry parked near the brothel. She thought he was going to walk her home, but he didn't. "Aren't you taking me back?"

Harry grimaced. "No, and don't ask me to take you home, because that's as good as an invitation. Stay with me tonight."

"What's wrong with all of you?" Miriam complained. "Why does everything have to be so base?"

Harry scanned her face. "Nothing will happen. You'll be perfectly safe, but I want to talk to you. We haven't really spoken before and I want to see what kind of girl Sinjen likes. I admit, he's got a better eye for beauty than I do. I like everything to be packaged nicely first, if you know what I mean, but I think Sinjen sees a certain charm in everyone."

Miriam frowned as Harry led her to the rooms he'd rented at Carol's. Varkov, now Volkov, wasn't there. The room was decorated in Queen Anne style, warm and opulent. There was a yellow furniture suite arranged around low tables. The room was well-lit but didn't have any windows or a fireplace. Instead, it was heated by radiators, in both this room and the adjoining smaller room, which contained a carved wooden bed.

Champagne on ice was waiting for him, and hot marrow on toast was brought in once they arrived, as well as some caviar. "I have to say, Sinjen was right about Carol too. She's wonderful. It seems like she can get ahold of just about everything, and now I'm half in love with her myself. I think this whole establishment is a bit of a hidden gem, though I know coin makes a difference." Miriam didn't react to his praise; it did seem fair. Not that she could verify it for herself, or would want to.

He gestured for Miriam to sit down. She sat on a comfortable chair, while Harry lay across a chaise lounge. She felt a little too intimidated to look at him, her eyes following the floral pattern on the rug instead. He poured a glass for her and directed her attention to the food.

Miriam spread some of the marrow onto buttered toast. It was delicious, and nicely peppered, but she wanted to cry.

"Goodness me, what could have happened to upset you?" Harry asked, and made sure her drink was topped up all the way. Miriam told him.

Harry laughed. "Well, I can ask Carlotta about Richard. She tends to keep a close eye on Sinjen, which is very sensible. As to the rest, you can't take anything Sinjen does too seriously. He probably would have you as his mistress, from what he's said to me, but I think he was only trying to get a rise out of you. He *is* the type to test affection. His whole life relies on knowing what he can and can't get away with.

He's had a rough night, even before we returned to Whitby. I can't tell you the details. You wouldn't want to know, and he wouldn't want you to, but the way he was when you saw him at the house was very typical. He has had a freedom recently that he's never really had before, not since he died. Even so, I can't believe how different he is from what I'd expected." He spread some caviar onto toast for her, as she'd been looking at it with scepticism.

She ate it cautiously and seemed to enjoy it, so he continued. "I once met a very unfortunate woman, little more than a girl at the time, really. I had sympathy for the little thing, but she didn't fully take my interest at first. She was so wretched, and too young besides. She was ragged, dirty and very ill-used." Miriam looked up at him, eyes widening.

Harry explained, "I took her in, I couldn't stand to leave her to the streets. In time, she grew into a very fine young lady, at least in appearance. Though she earned her keep, in my eyes, giving me someone to dote on when I remembered to, she was still a problem for the rest of the household.

She kept sleeping around, she'd sneak out, she'd get into fights, she was just generally impulsive and wild. One day, I was told by the matron that she'd had quite enough of this girl. I'd forbidden that she could be turned out, so a direct complaint was the only option. When she was brought to me, all I saw was a great beauty, with eyes full of sadness, anger and hurt. I admit, I was taken with her at once."

Miriam added a little more caviar to her toast, as Harry smiled indulgently. "What is the point of this tale?" she asked, glancing at the door.

"I'm getting to it. The girl became a great favourite of mine. I could hardly bear to watch her suffer, but her spirit and will to live was remarkable. One day, she accused me of poisoning her, and I was so shocked that I had to lie down."

"Why?" Miriam asked, too concerned to eat.

Harry reminded her to drink, and she did. "Because I was killing her. I thought she hadn't brought it up because it was obvious, and she was hoping not to make me kill her faster. I don't like it when they don't trust me, you see. My servants would know that. My distress came from the fact that the girl had never even been told *what* she worked for. She'd been kept in the dark by the others. She had been, in effect, marked for death, kept as an outsider since she'd arrived. Even in my house, she'd never had a friend. Besides me, arguably, but I was murdering her."

"So you let her go?" Miriam asked.

"Good heavens, no. I killed her, but I did turn her. I thought the dear little thing deserved a second chance at life. She's been a capable vampire, but she, to this day, isn't much better than Sinjen when it comes to her body. One day, I asked her why, and *this* is the point of my story."

Miriam stared at him. He noted how pretty she was in dark blue, and how girlish. She had a serious set to her jaw and brow, but the softer style of dress brought out her large dark eyes and warm complexion.

He sighed. "She said she had never felt she owned her body. It was like it didn't belong to her, and so she no longer cared who made use of it. It was one of the most tragic things I'd ever heard." Miriam's eyes widened, and she looked very sweet. "Sinjen is like that too. Carlotta tells me that he was once perfect. Moral to a fault, in life, but he would have gone mad by now, if he was still that way. He still has his resolve, it's terrifying, actually. He makes such slow progress, but he keeps going and never gives up. He's got some goal and he'll make it happen. He's one of the most dangerous, calculating and ruthless vampires that I've ever met."

Miriam blinked. She ate a little more toast and thought carefully. "I've never seen any sign of something like that. I don't think I believe you."

Harry roared with laughter. "Okay, don't believe me."

"Why men? Why is he like that?" she asked, waving her hands. "Was it me?"

Harry smiled at her. "I promise you, no."

They ate and talked for a long time. Harry was charming and attentive, and it was hard not to want to be near him. He was easygoing, even excessively so, but there was something about him that made her uneasy.

He was so painfully handsome that it became hard to nail down the reason for her discomfort. Except by being what he was, which he could not help. Harry had an honesty about him, and a genuine sweetness to his smile.

"Will you be safe if you sleep here?" Miriam asked.

"I should think so. They gave me the key to the door," Harry said, relaxing in his chair. She raised an eyebrow, so he added, "I'm not entirely helpless, even in the day. Not all of us are."

Miriam stood and went to leave for the night, but he took her hand. "I don't want you thinking you aren't desirable," he whispered, drawing her closer.

She risked touching his hand as he held her against him, her pulse racing. He brushed her hair back from her neck. She shivered.

"It's cold tonight, do you really want to go out again? Why don't you stay here with me?" he asked, close to her ear.

Miriam wanted to leave, but it really was comfortable there and Harry was very hard to turn down. She wasn't sure she'd ever seen a better-looking man. He turned her to face him and kissed her lips.

His kiss had been gentle, but she hadn't recoiled. She tentatively touched his cheek, wondering if he could genuinely find her attractive, when he could have anyone. He smiled. Harry kissed her again, more deeply, and led her to the bedroom.

Tansy Poisoning

Chapter 26

Once Miriam had left, Sinjen couldn't settle down or concentrate on his letters. Jack came over and put his hands on his shoulders. Sinjen shook him off and told him to keep away from his desk.

"Oh? I thought I was yours?" Jack said. "And you know I don't read all that well."

Sinjen relaxed a little. "I've got a lot on my mind, and I don't like Miriam and Harry together. I'm going to speak to Carlotta." He stood quickly, patted Jack's arm and went to Carlotta's door.

He knocked and was called in. Carlotta was lounging on her bed with Tansy, leaning close together. They were reading a book to each other. Both pretty, slender and long-limbed.

He sat on the end of her bed and sulked. Eventually, Carlotta asked him what was wrong. Tansy chuckled. Sinjen didn't want to speak, but flopped onto her mattress and rested his head on her legs.

She sighed. "Is it that bad?" He pressed his face into her dress and moaned. "Can you give me a clue?"

"Harry and Miriam," he complained.

"I can't say. How well do you think I know him?" Carlotta sighed. "Do you, Tansy?"

"Actually, no, not that well. To me, he's fairly young, and Southern Cross was quite mobile. He was the envoy between Tigers-Eye and Southern Cross, later Moonlight, for a big section of their international trade but, frankly, he was useless. The only thing he did before ignoring all his responsibilities was enthrall a really competent official. He was even turned, because Harry didn't want to replace him. In the end he joined Tigers-Eye instead of Penumbra, and Harry made himself redundant. Then he practically moved into his opium den. People didn't see him for decades."

Carlotta frowned. "So, he's..."

"He says laziness is just a highly evolved form of efficiency," Tansy explained. "He also said that time is our most valuable resource and that explains his priorities. I did have to try and keep him on track at one time, you see. He actually wasn't unreliable; at least, his clerk wasn't. In the end I just left him to it. There wasn't anything that could be done to improve him. He was an immovable object in that regard."

"But Miss Miriam?" Sinjen asked. "I don't want her hurt."

"A little pet?" Carlotta sighed.

"That's not an unfair assessment."

Carlotta stroked his hair. "Alright. I'll let you know if I find out."

A thrall knocked on the door and told Carlotta she had a phone call. Sinjen let her get up, then lay on the pillow next to Tansy.

227

She rested her head on his chest and neatened his collar. The motion sent a very pleasant shiver down his spine. "Did you want something else?" Tansy asked. Her voice was wonderfully soft.

"Yes. I've been hearing a lot about a ring recently. Lord Petri has a bounty out on it, and I wondered if you might remember it?"

"How old do you think I am?" she asked, affecting offence.

"Do you really want me to answer that?" Sinjen laughed. "I have asked around."

She giggled, and ran her fingers down the buttons on his chest. "The red one?"

"Yes. Would you know what it looked like, exactly?" he asked.

"Sure. It's Roman, much older even than Petri. Gold, with a large carnelian gem on top showing carved tansy flowers, it's very prettily done. The old stone had cracked, you see."

He kissed her hair. "In that case, was it a gift for your wedding?"

"It was. Unfortunately, it was lost in transit. I should have had it on my person, I suppose it's gone for good."

"Then it's yours?" Sinjen asked.

"Technically, I suppose it is, but Elder Petri put the bounty on it. So, if it's ever found, it might as well be given to him. I imagine it'll turn up somewhere odd and puzzle an archaeologist one day." Her tone had been sad, but she'd been looking at him throughout.

For the moment, she'd become so enchanting that he couldn't re-member the reasons he'd heard to stay away from her.

"Who were you marrying?" he asked.

Tansy frowned. "Mind your own business."

"That bad, huh?" Sinjen laughed. She smacked his chest and went to sit up. "Wait. Is this it?" He produced the ring from his pocket and showed it to her.

Her mouth fell open. She took it and turned it over in her hands.

"How on earth did you manage that?"

She examined it carefully, and her hands trembled. "Let me show you something." She twisted the ring and it opened. "Oh, it still has the poison inside it."

Her voice had been very casual, but Sinjen retreated to the edge of the bed. "Sorry, how bad was this marriage?" he asked.

She laughed at him and shut it. "You can see now why Petri might have wanted this ring back. Or at least, why he gave it to me."

He nodded. Tansy was, in her own way, quite feared. He'd have to find out more about her, but this did get more difficult as vampires aged. In general, the older ones didn't swap stories about one another, and they were hard to get to know well. She handed the ring back to him and kissed him on the cheek. "It's amazing that you found it. I'll keep an eye on you," she said, as Sinjen went back to his room. He hadn't sensed any risk from Tansy, but if people ever did, she wouldn't be considered dangerous.

He wrote a letter to Lord Petri, enclosed the ring in the envelope, then sealed it.

He gave it to Jack. "I need you to leave tomorrow at dawn and take this to Elder Petri, in person. You won't arrive in daylight anyway, so he should be available." Jack nodded. Sinjen wrote a few more letters out and gave them to him as well. "And, would you post these too? Lady Eliza will be home at some point after tomorrow night. It may be safer if you aren't home then, anyway."

Jack examined the letters. One was to Nightfall Castle and contained two envelopes. One was being sent to Italy, to someone named Arlo.

The last was to Miriam, but it was still on his desk. Jack frowned.

Sinjen stood and kissed him. "I haven't forgotten you." He was about to ask Jack to take his whip off, so he didn't touch it by accident, when there was a knock on the door.

Sinjen sighed. He also had a phone call.

Harry was on the phone; it was so close to dawn. "Oh, Sinjen. Can you come and pick up your Miriam? I can't be bothered to take her home. I'm going to kick her out in a little bit, because I need to rest."

"Where is she?" he asked.

"My room at Carol's. Quite unconscious."

"Harry, did you hurt her?" Sinjen asked, afraid.

"Oh, good heavens, no. The little thing just drank too much and, well, she's tired. I can't exactly leave her on the floor of a brothel, though, can I? I'd get a reputation. Volkov is here, by the way. Do you want to say hello?"

"No. I'll send someone to collect her. Wake her up in a few minutes." Sinjen hung up and leant against the wall. He raked his fingers though his hair, thinking it would really be better if Harry had some brains.

He went back to Jack, apologised that he would be sleeping away tonight and kissed him. Jack had taken off the whip and embraced Sinjen for a few minutes. "I do have to go. I'll see you when you come back. Take this before you leave." He went to his desk and pulled out a new pendant. He put it around Jack's neck. It had a fox on one side, with stars behind it, while on the back was a pretty cathedral.

"What's this?"

"That should let Penumbra know you belong to me, a Nightfall vampire. It would be foolish for me to let you go without it, because it should stop them from eating you. Bring the whip too, obviously. Can you use it? I have easier weapons."

"I know what I'm doing," Jack grinned. "Some of the girls taught me, years ago, just for fun really."

"Oh, I see." Sinjen laughed. He kissed him again and spirited to Richard's cottage.

That was just about all he had time to do tonight. He explained to Richard that he'd need to go and collect Miriam. He would be asleep in the basement when he got back. He asked him to pay close attention to her wellbeing.

When Miriam was awake, Richard helped her dress again. He'd done a little of that before he woke her, so she wouldn't be too embarrassed.

Harry was already tiring and losing patience. Volkov seemed happier, but would still be exhausting.

She was quite drunk, and clung to his arm, but gripped the door frame before she left. She turned to Volkov. "I need to know," she slurred, "those two women who died. Was it you, or the fledgling?"

"It wasn't me," Volkov said, "I don't kill women if I can help it. Not outdoors, anyway, but I was watching the fledgling and I did see him kill the first woman. You know, the one before you found him."

"He said that was you," Miriam insisted.

"Well, he would. I'm sure it was very embarrassing for him. His pride would have been wounded by hiring a whore in the first place, and then by stooping to killing her." Volkov considered her rather sadly, and watched Richard escort her out.

"Where do you want to go?" Richard asked when they were outside.

"Your cottage," she said, her eyes growing misty.

He brought Miriam to a cab and followed it back to the cottage. He didn't think she was in the right condition to ride double.

She was weeping quietly by the time they arrived, so he paid the driver and escorted her into the house.

Sinjen was still waiting, having a smoke. He came over and examined her. "How much did you drink?"

"Maybe four glasses," she replied.

He frowned. "Is that a lot for you?"

"Yes, I think so."

He nodded, turned her face in his hands and wiped a tear from her eye. He went to the basement without saying anything else.

Miriam started to cry when he left. Richard chuckled.

"Why are you laughing?" she said, through tears.

"It's a little bit funny. Are you feeling guilty about taking Harry to bed? Because I don't even like men and I'd be a little tempted by that one."

"Why the hell would you say that to me?" she said, devolving into sobs.

Richard tried not to laugh more, and held her, even though she tried to push him away at first. "What is the matter?"

"I saw you kissing him!" Miriam wept.

"Who? Harry?" Richard asked, and she smacked his arm. "Sinjen!? No. I assure you, you didn't."

232

Miriam tried to pull away and he let her. She stood on the other side of the room, angrily wiping away tears.

"He's practically my father. If you... if you saw us in the garden, earlier, I can only imagine that you saw something out of its proper context. He, well... You've seen how enthusiastic his moods can get. He only wanted some affection. I know it's a little strange and embarrassing. Well. No. I won't say embarrassing, after all he's done for me. I-I don't mind if he demands attention now and then. It's not my cup of tea, exactly, but he said he'd just been shot." Richard's cheeks had turned a very pretty shade of pink.

"How old are you?" Miriam asked.

"I'm twenty-nine. Sinjen says I look older because I worry about him too much." He frowned and ran his fingers through the grey streaks at his temples.

Miriam sat down on one of the chairs and stared at the ceiling. "Do you think less of me? I feel so ashamed. I didn't know Harry could be so charming and I, Sinjen... He said something earlier that..."

"He can be terribly perceptive." Richard sighed. "What was it?"

"He put it shockingly, but he was right. I do want a family. I've been alone for so long."

Richard was struck, and sat down. "You're alone too?"

Neither of them could quite look at the other and sat in silence, listening to the wind blow leaves around outside.

Richard continued, "I have Sinjen. He's not a human. I suppose it doesn't make him less, but in a sense he feels rather removed from life. I know he cares for me, but he's... he's not a parent, he's not an old man. He's young forever and has no real need of a child, in the truest sense. God willing, I'll die before he does. I know what he is. I know he's done things I'd hang a human for, even if there was no law at all, but I also know *him*. He's... not evil, not all the time. What he *does* is evil.

I'm not certain which is worse. Sometimes I wonder if someone who was truly evil only did good things, even if he felt no joy or love from it... suppose it was duty or convention that motivated him, would that be goodness?" He took a long slow breath to marinade with his thoughts. "And his circumstances are not in his control."

"What if he died?" Miriam asked.

"Either of us could kill him," Richard pointed out. "Do you feel that it's right that he should die?"

"My feelings? In my soul... no, but on paper..."

"Is it wrong that we feel that? It's a certainty that more people will die if he lives."

Miriam didn't have the sense that he meant that they should kill him. He was only stating fact. "Would either thing be wrong?"

"For me?" Richard laughed. "Tomorrow, he will give this house to me. I'll be established, perhaps not in any great sense. This house is large enough, if still unsuitable for a big family, and my garden is enough to feed me year round, even turn a little profit. It's much more than I'd have had without him, in all likelihood. I have no reason to harm him. Yet, this would be the fairest time for him to die, if I were to decide. It would seem wrong to wait until tomorrow, I mean."

Miriam rubbed an eyebrow with one hand. "Me too. I feel like he wants something from me that I can't define. I feel like he'd take care of me, even if I were, forgive me... to ask for money. I-I don't think it would bother him, but I'm a woman, not a man. I don't know what a man in my position would do. Perhaps negotiate some absurd allowance..."

Richard smiled at her. "He'd probably pay it. He's done well for himself, and I'm sure he'd ask for little in return. You aren't asking me to help you negotiate?"

"Good grief, no, I could never. I'm only saying. I wouldn't, but I know I can't benefit myself here, maybe that's why he likes me. So, if I did, then..."

Richard shrugged. "I think he wants you to marry me."

Miriam flushed. "I forgot."

He laughed. "Come to bed with me."

Miriam's eyes widened.

"Because I'm no Harry?" he said, but he was still smiling.

"I like you more than Harry," Miriam admitted, "but I've debased myself; you can't want me."

Richard laughed again. "I'm not a boy. I'm a grown man, I've done enough foolish things myself. I don't think you're somehow immune from life, just because you're a woman. We don't have to do anything. Only hold me, alright?"

Miriam felt like she might cry again. "Okay." She took his hand and led him up to her room.

She undressed him, partially, and found that his body was quite lovely. His skin was hot and soft; in spite of his careworn expression, he'd clearly been well cared for and never suffered major harm.

She kissed him, and let him embrace her and warm her under the sheets.

To Meet Again

Chapter 27

Richard and Miriam were home when Sinjen woke up. They looked a bit tired, but otherwise happy.

Miriam left when his solicitor arrived, and asked Sinjen to meet her at her house later.

He turned up with some new blankets as she was tidying away her books. She'd bought a new bookshelf and given away her old one.

"Oh, that's nice," Sinjen said with a contented smile as he came in. "Nettie said to tell you that you have gotten a bit more interesting recently."

"I'm not sure it's been for the best," Miriam said, with a small frown. "I've been thinking about my association with you. Maybe a bit too much."

"Dear me. Have I done something wrong?" Sinjen asked.

"It's nothing that you've done, exactly. I think I've become a worse person, in very little time. Then, I was thinking about vampire novels and…"

"How we are a corrupting influence?" Sinjen asked.

"Are you?" She put the last of the books on the shelf and turned to him. Her forehead was furrowed.

"You're too young for expressions like that. You'll end up grey before your time."

"It's not my hair I'm concerned about!" she said, exasperated.

"I understand." Sinjen sat down on her bed, and considered her seriously. "There are a few factors, I suppose, as to the question of whether exposure to vampires is necessarily a corrupting force. For example: can I help it or not? Why is it this way? And can you do anything about your own morality? Are those the kinds of questions?"

"Yes. I think so. Also, is this something… that vampires enjoy?" Miriam asked, wringing a loose scrap of paper in her hands.

Sinjen smiled, but his face was harder than usual. "Yes, they do, most of us. I don't, but I suppose you won't believe me." Miriam didn't look like she believed him at all, but came over and sat next to him. She studied his face as he went on. "As evidence, Richard Wright, who has known me for the vast majority of his life, is decent, isn't he? He has his flaws, I know. He's a little prone to gambling. I do overpay him, so he has to do something with it, but in all likelihood his—"

Miriam sighed. "He's overly affectionate?"

"Is he?" Sinjen asked with a mischievous smile. "In all fairness, that *is* very likely our fault. Vampire society is rather decadent and prone to boredom." A very tired expression came over him, and Miriam remembered that a lot of his duties pertained to entertainment.

"I don't know if that's because we are cursed, or if it's only because we are old, and the clans are excessively wealthy. I was a little bit worried for him in his early twenties, but he did improve as he grew older. I don't think he was very well-suited to the environment, and my fear for his safety led me to retire him earlier than usual. I only ever have one personal thrall. That isn't something I like either, but it *is* necessary.

Losing him would be more than I could stand. He's honest, sensible and stable, but just as there are vampires who see innocence and want to destroy it, there are others who love nothing more than to disturb a peaceful mind. In my opinion anyway, either of those things could be for the good in the end, but that's not what I'm talking about. I mean, that there are vampires who see mental stability and goodness and will seek to fully destroy whoever holds them."

Miriam shuddered. "And what do you do?"

Sinjen half smiled. "I'm just a bad influence. I have bad habits and I suffer 'at home.' Sometimes, I can't help bringing that around with me. I don't mean to, but I'm not, in the slightest, unique in that. They say misery loves company. Well, I want the people I love to be happy, but when I'm disturbed, I can..."

"Cause a disturbance?" Miriam suggested.

"I'm told I can be a little bit temperamental."

Miriam couldn't help it, and laughed behind her hand. "So. Did we solve our mystery?"

Sinjen chuckled. "The mystery of who glassed some thugs? I'd say so."

"Sum it up for me," she said, laughing. "Do it like Sherlock Holmes."

He grinned and drew himself up. "My dear Miriam! We did solve the mystery. Though the assailant was the vampire hunter Alexander Varkov the fifth, the true cause of the disturbance was his great-grandfather, now a vampire, Alexander the second!"

She giggled. "No, go on, tell me properly. I want to make sure we are on the same page."

"Oh, alright," he said with a smile. "This is it, though. Alexander five, upon learning that he had a child, I imagine, grew fearful for his wife and son. Let's call her his wife, because by their own will the two would have been wed. And, they did have a son."

"I'd call them married," Miriam admitted.

"Me too, I hate a tragic romance. The cause of this fear was a vampire going by the name Victor Bickerstaff. The story he had fed the family was that he was the last survivor of a very hated clan."

Miriam gasped. "But I was told they were a romantic clan."

Sinjen turned to her in stunned surprise, then blinked. "Well, um, yes. I suppose they were, at first." He took a deep breath, his expression conflicted. "In the beginning, and this lasted a few centuries, they were popular and served a purpose. They were viewed as a rather whimsical clan, as vampires go, and were a little over-indulged. They'd arrange marriages and draw up contracts between spouses, the view being that marriage was a business agreement, of sorts. Though there was nothing to stop any other kind of arrangement, or manner of separation. Including murder, which has always been a popular option."

Miriam's mouth fell open.

"I know. What ended them, though, was their failure to grant divorces. They were wiped out, in very short order, after they started to deny those."

Miriam's eyes were so wide that Sinjen became mildly concerned that they'd fall or dry out.

"Anyway," Sinjen continued, suppressing his amusement, "Bickerstaff was not really from Star-Cross. He was Alexander Varkov the second, killed by Harry not long before my own clan was destroyed. He ended up with a vampiric bounty, but they issued it believing he was a human. So, as long as they don't find out his true identity, it shouldn't be a problem. It's expired now, really, but I can't ask about it without raising suspicions. He also earnt a human bounty for himself, as a vampire. He faked his death, made his Bickerstaff identity, and was killing the other Varkovs so that they would not continue to hunt him. They, of course, knew he had turned."

Miriam sighed. "No, he told me, at first, maybe he was. Afterwards, it was for the thrill of the fight. So, his costume was just so that he could fight them without them recognising him. Alexander the fourth probably suspects who he is, though. Perhaps he remembers his grandfather affectionately, I suppose that's common enough, so he hasn't told anyone."

Sinjen looked up at the ceiling and took a deep breath. "You see? You see what I have to deal with? Vampires are all mad. Am I, Miriam?"

She didn't look certain. "Sinjen." She took his hand and kissed it lightly. She looked so sweet and compassionate that his heart softened.

"I'd make you my lover. Perhaps that's foolish, but I would."

It seemed she was about to say something, but couldn't quite bring herself to.

"No. I know it's wrong. I just want to be close to you, or to someone." She concealed her feelings about this and looked at her hands. "You don't have to hide how you feel about that. You don't think I'm evil for it, do you?"

Miriam turned to face him. "I don't think love is wrong, but I also don't think we always know our own desires. I certainly... don't seem to. I know I got angry at you for deciding what you think I could handle, and now I'm doing the same, but... they say male desire is greater than a woman's."

Sinjen smiled. "I think they also say a woman's satisfaction is greater." She looked puzzled. "Is that so? Why?"

He couldn't help laughing. "I could show you."

"No!" she cried.

Sinjen did his best to suppress his amusement. "Miriam, you're wonderful... Well, anyway. Alexander two didn't care, then, for Varkov's bloodline. Only the fight. The second time he came for this man, he dealt a fatal blow."

Miriam nodded. Her expression was pained, but Sinjen was grinning. He steadied his breathing a little, then continued. "Then he watched the new vampire die at the hands of his own sect."

"Is that *fun* for you?" Miriam asked.

He laughed. "No, never, only the story is a little thrilling. Varkov five, in his dying breaths, begged me for a chance for vengeance, and to protect his son and wife. I obliged. I can't resist something like that, someone fighting to live with such sincerity. I've had to survive myself. I've done things you couldn't imagine."

He was doing his best to suppress his emotions, but it was very close to what she had seen in Varkov. Harry may have been right. It was like there was something Sinjen would do anything to accomplish; even thinking about it excited him.

"Then?" Miriam asked.

"Hmm? Nothing. Alexander had his fight, nobly, I admit, to show his son what life meant to them. I was shot. I assume everything went well with dear Viola?"

Miriam nodded. "Well enough in the circumstances." Some instinct told her to keep her mouth shut about the family.

"Well, is that all?" Sinjen asked.

Miriam gave him a very cold look.

"Did I miss something?"

"Yes," Miriam said, frostily. "The women."

"Which women?"

She raised an eyebrow. "The two who died. One when I found Varkov, and the other washed up on the beach. And the fisherman, but I think he was just in the wrong place at the wrong time."

"Oh." Sinjen sighed. "You didn't tell me, love. Varkov the fifth killed them?"

She looked revolted. "You knew about the one I whose body I heard discovered. It must have only been minutes after he'd done it, and it makes sense now. His expression and, maybe, why he came with me."

Sinjen objected. "I'm sorry, I was foolish. At that time, I believed Varkov's story. I neglected to consider her fate after we learnt more."

"Because you don't care about death!" Miriam cried. "I don't look so different to Viola, do I? Not as pretty, perhaps, but you know I'm out late. On some other day, it might have been me that they found in an alley."

Sinjen was hurt. "I... It never occurred to me. I would never have let you be harmed, but you never told me about the second one. I didn't know it was a pattern."

Miriam glared at him, her expression one of revulsion. "You knew he would need to eat, didn't you? Even if he might have... I don't believe you about animal blood. It's not the same, is it?"

Sinjen touched his lips. "No."

"It's cruel. Each day... your life is—"

"My life is stolen, Miriam." Sinjen sighed, putting his hands on her shoulders and kissing her cheek.

He felt her heartbeat quicken. "That is the curse I live under. I'll make you a promise. I'll leave myself asleep in your care, again, at times. If you see me commit murder, or prove to yourself that I deserve death, then kill me. I will do nothing to prevent you, not that I could."

Miriam looked at him. He did not meet her eye. He was so handsome, but his face remained stony. "What about me?"

His brow furrowed. "What about you?"

She stood up and ushered him out of her room.

"Miriam," he sighed, "you need to know something. I don't think I will see you for a long while. Can I write to you?" He looked a little pleading.

She kissed his lips, and immediately regretted it. "Then, I will see you another time," she said, and shut the door.

In a moment, he knocked again. "I forgot to give you this. Compensation for your time and assistance, and this too, which is from Varkov. He was quite horrified to learn that his descendant had stolen some clothes, so he asked me to repay the dress shop for him. Family honour, I suppose."

He left before she could say anything about her fee. He'd given her a letter, and a slightly absurd cheque.

Miriam read it in her room and smiled. It was the stupidest letter she'd ever received, but if it amused Sinjen then she'd indulge him:

Miss Miriam, I have very little free time, and require you to be available for various capers. As you might imagine, there is some difficulty solving mysteries when I can only move around at night. Please only take the kind of work that would leave you available to travel. Lots of love, Sinjen.

Sinjen wandered away into the night and his mood started to darken. He was hailing a cab when Harry and Volkov stepped out towards him. He could hardly have looked less impressed.

"Why the long face, dear chap?" Harry asked. He had Volkov by the shoulder. The two looked happy with their evening.

"My mistress is home tonight," Sinjen said icily.

"Oh, yes." Harry yawned. "I suppose she is."

"How nice that you get to be away for it. I suppose you'll be off to Italy again soon?"

Harry smiled. "Of course. I must look after my dear baby boy."

Volkov frowned, unsatisfied. "I've been surviving alone for over a century."

"No, you haven't," Sinjen sighed. "You're just an innocent little fledgling. You need to act that way. We can do nothing to protect you beyond that. You've committed to a very big lie."

Volkov looked between them both and only saw coldness. "I'll do my best."

"Your life depends on it," Sinjen reminded him. "Hopefully, if you cock it up, it won't come back to bite us as well."

They climbed into the carriage. It was a little ragged, but they didn't care. Harry even left enough money under a cushion that the driver could have the whole cab neatened up.

Sinjen hadn't yet gone inside when a large carriage arrived, pulled by black horses. A few vampires came out to watch its approach. Sinjen had been smoking, and had finished off two cigarettes already.

The driver went to let the occupant out. He bowed deeply, already terrified.

"Stand," a soft voice instructed.

Sinjen looked up to see Laura. The rest of the carriage was empty. He suppressed his relief, in case word might make it back to Eliza. "My Eliza is not home?" he asked, sounding dejected. Laura's face fell.

"No, Sinjen. She only sent me back to inform you that you are to return to Nightfall at once, with the rest of her belongings."

Sinjen's expression turned to horror. "My new thrall is not ready yet. I need one more night."

Laura laughed. "Then, you'll be happy to hear, I made excellent progress on my journey. We can leave tomorrow night, in haste, and it will all be the same."

Sinjen took her hands. "You must be tired, little darling. Come in, I'll run you a bath and send for a well-fed thrall."

She kissed his cheek. "Thank you, Sinjen."

Seeing that Eliza was not home, most of the vampires who had come out to meet her had already cleared away. He checked in with Sora on his way upstairs and told her to mind the house in their absence.

When Laura was in his room, and no one else, he kissed her passionately, caressing her and encouraging her towards the bed. She let him push her down without resistance.

"Master," she whispered, and for a moment he froze. He'd thought his fledgling was dead. He'd forgotten that he'd had another. "Dear master, what is it?"

He exhaled lightly near her ear. "Dear Laura."

"I don't think I want to be called Laura," she confessed, kissing his cheek.

"What is your full name?"

"Laura Leonard," she said. "But is it a little plain?"

"Perhaps," he admitted, kissing down her cheek and neck. He heard her gasp, and felt her chest heave. He pressed his lips against her sternum. "You know why male vampires don't have daughters, like the women do?"

A soft moan escaped her lips. "You're my maker. Choose what you want."

He pressed his lips against hers; they were soft and full. "You're tempting me."

She let out a cold hard laugh and rolled him over, so that she was on top of him. "No. We are both only toys, it seems. Show me what you like, and when you are done, you'd better point me at whoever you want dead. I didn't like you out of sympathy. I liked you because I could see the hatred in your eyes whenever you thought no one saw your face.

I don't want Eliza to live. I don't want anyone who hurt you to live. I want to serve your ambition. You have no one in your corner, but I will be, dear master."

Sinjen gasped and held her tightly against him. "My own dear fledgling. You haven't the slightest idea how much that means to me."

In the small hours the phone rang.

Sinjen kissed Laura again, wrapped himself in a dressing gown and went to answer the phone. "Good morning." He yawned.

Elder Petri laughed. "Good morning, Sinjen."

"Oh my. Good morning, Lord Petri. Is my thrall alright?"

Petri sounded amused. "Jack is very well. He is rather an amusing young man, and I won't mind in the slightest if you tried to turn him. I assume he's new, or he wouldn't have tried to pick my pocket."

"Oh no. Did he? It's part of why I like him, but—"

He could hear Petri was smiling when he responded, "It's nothing to worry about, I only had a couple of prunes in there. That was because I'd toured the gardens. It's not some absurd euphemism."

Sinjen snorted, then apologised. "That's entirely understandable. I'm quite keen on dried apple slices myself. It was the correct ring?"

"It was. I'm delighted. How on earth did you find it?"

"It was in the possession of a member of the Wolfsbane sect. It was only by chance that Sir Balcom let me know it was sought after. May I ask your advice? I asked Lady Tansy if she knew of it, and I showed it to her, but will that cause me any risk?"

He sounded afraid, but Petri did not mind. "No, Mister Carlyle. Lady Tansy is very sweet, but her reputation has suffered badly over the years. I will tell her that you are my friend and no harm will come to you. Be good to her and she will be the same. She is... Well, in time, perhaps you will get to know her."

"Thank you, Lord Petri," he said, with considerable relief.

"As for me... have you told anyone of this? Your letter suggested not, but your mistress..."

"No, Lord Petri. She is away, by some small miracle." He was momentarily afraid for himself. No Eliza meant that he was without her protection, and it wasn't impossible that Petri might want to silence him.

"I am not permitted to show favouritism. Lady Chloe, however, *was* a favourite of mine, and a woman of honour. I had no objection in the slightest to her choice of husband. Do you remember her well?" Petri asked.

"I do, but I did not know her very well. She was always good to me. I remember her warm smile, but in truth, I had very little time with her, and there was so much upheaval."

He heard Petri sigh. "She was remarkable. I fear that few remember her as she deserved to be remembered. I do recall, though, her speaking to me of her excitement and hope for her new fledgling. Daylight was a highly exclusive group."

Sinjen struggled to keep the emotion from his voice. "I can't tell you how much joy it brings me to hear someone speak well of my family. I had such a short time with them, only Margaret..."

"She's a merit to us. Before her..." Petri sighed, "After..."

"I know, Lord Petri. It's a wonder she turned out the way she did. My... beloved Eliza..." Here he could not entirely conceal the disgust in his voice. "She was so similar in circumstance, only fifteen instead of twelve, when she—"

"No, don't say more, Sinjen. It's too shameful, and I remember those days. Exceptionally young wives did fall out of fashion, thank goodness. Thank you, at any rate. You've made a friend, and I'll show you by concealing the reward. That should be useful to someone in your position – your property has been seized once or twice already, hasn't it?" Sinjen confirmed that it had been. "Good, then I can be useful and manage this for you, until you have time to visit me in person. Would that suit you?"

"That sounds perfect," he agreed.

When he'd hung up, he sat for a few minutes to process things. This couldn't have worked out better. Lady Tansy and Lord Petri were now his friends, and he'd never heard that Petri was prone to deception.

He had his own loyal fledgling, and she was cunning.

He'd have to speak to Volkov when he could, because it wasn't impossible that he might turn out to be useful.

Killing Harry still might be sensible, but he had been an ally, so there wasn't a rush. Even his new thrall had been well received.

The only downside was that he'd have to return to Nightfall, but he needed to for the Ancient, anyway, so it wasn't wise to avoid it.

They left the next night, in the carriage Laura had arrived in. It was one of Eliza's favourites and very comfortable, so Eliza must like her. Jack was on his right and Laura was to his left. He felt safe with both and put his arms around them, letting them lean against either shoulder.

"I'll tell you all about Nightfall, Jack. Laura, you won't be bored, I hope," he said, kissing her head.

"No, I have been out of my depth. I've had to cling to Eliza; she hasn't taught me much, except how to serve her better. That has been painful, actually."

Sinjen sighed. "Unfortunately, you heal better now, so she'll have more fun. You haven't told anyone that I'm your maker, have you?"

"Good heavens, no. I'm not an idiot, that would be embarrassing." Jack bristled at this, but didn't say anything.

"No, that's very sensible. You might as well say it was Harry who turned you, that won't surprise anyone. You'll be more useful to me if people think we have no association with one another. Would that bother you?"

"No, not much," Laura admitted, "But you do love me?"

"Of course, I couldn't be happier with you," he said, holding her tighter to him. She beamed. Jack traced a pattern on his leg, and he held him more tightly too. "It's safer if people never find out that I care for either of you as I do," Sinjen said, and for the rest of the journey, he told them everything that he could imagine might be useful.

Letter to my Readers

Dear reader,

I'm the author. I've been talking this whole time, but using the voice in your head. I'm told that indie authors like myself should leave a note like this, so please humour me. Thank you so much for taking the time to read my book. It means the whole world to me, especially if you liked it, and I hope you did.

I'm new to all of this. I started writing a couple of years ago, and first published in June 2023. I'm still figuring out how publishing independently works. It's all a bit of trial and error, I've definitely made mistakes, but I'm really enjoying it. That said, it's not the same as traditional publishing, and building an audience is one of the biggest difficulties.

To that end; if you've made it this far, and you've had fun, please consider leaving me a nice review on Amazon, Goodreads or wherever. It makes a huge difference to authors like me, it really does. Not only does it encourage other readers to take a chance on us, it also makes us very happy and motivates us to keep going.

There are all kinds of other little things that matter to us too. Being spoken about and recommended is great. Even using the perks Amazon provides can help us inch up in the rankings. For example, using free KDP downloads and Audible credits. Prime even lets you get pre-released books for free. And of course, if you're interested in finding my new and upcoming releases and hearing my writing news, I have:

My blog, where I talk about what's going on, and some other random things. Following me there also means Wordpress emails you when I post something:

https://michaelbchikondi.wordpress.com/

My Twitter and Facebook, where I do the same:

https://twitter.com/M_B_Chikondi

https://www.facebook.com/profile.php?id=100093515463231

And if you're a reviewer, and you'd like a hard copy of one of my books, just let me know. I'm not above trading treats for attention.

Also, here's my email: michael_chikondi@hotmail.com

And that's it, thank you so much for your time. Have a wonderful day, and don't be eaten by vampires or anything.

Sincerely,

Michael B. Chikondi

Also By

Michael B. Chikondi

Creeping Fate

-Technically a prequel

Idle Hands: The Mystery Game

Peview

It was a magnificent candlelit meal, a full spread of intricately prepared dishes, many of them recipes that Queen Victoria's chefs had created for her. They were a little ridiculous. The soup in front of him was a clear beef broth containing vegetables cut into flowers, shapes and stars, but this sort of thing amused Lady Eliza. He watched her. With her dark, carefully styled hair, dark eyes and petite figure, she was wonderfully dressed in every regard. In spite of her hatred for both the look and style of this decade's clothing, she'd mastered it. It was like the entire era only existed to serve her. She was delicate in appearance but did not have especially pleasant features. She turned to her neighbour and he struggled not to show his fear. He forced a not-too terrified laugh at her quip and she adjusted her lace sleeve before stabbing her soup with a delicate gold fork.

Sinjen had spent weeks putting this party together for her. She'd loved every moment. Her favourite vampires and vampiresses were here, though he doubted she even really knew who they were or why they tolerated her. He'd given her everything: her favourite music, food, diversions and perversions. She could hardly be happier.

"Mistress?" he asked.

"Sinjen?" she breathed, examining a heart-shaped carrot with the appropriate degree of revulsion and a small smile.

"May I go on holiday for a fortnight?"

The sounds in the room ceased and, though no one appeared to be looking at him, it was very apparent that the vampire guests were listening intently.

"Why would you want a holiday?" Eliza asked, and bit the heart in half.

"I thought it would be fun, dear Mistress. It might be nice to travel. As much as it would pain me to be away from you, I think I'd really enjoy a little change of scenery."

The room was silent. Someone dropped a fork, the sound echoing through the room, but the vampire in question didn't risk picking it up.

"And why would you *want* a change?" Eliza asked, her voice and aspect chilling. She gave a slight nod to the candle between Sinjen and herself and he wordlessly held his hand over it.

"I haven't travelled for a long time, dear Mistress," he replied, the pain he felt barely creeping into his voice, though it was apparent to her from his eyes.

"And you want to?" she asked, her voice even harder. "Why?"

He gasped, but continued, ignoring the agony, "I thought you might let me. As a little gift."

She leant back and considered him. She blinked slowly at his hand and he lifted it to show her the burn. She shook her head, and he held it over the flame again. "As a *gift*, you want time away from *me*?"

"Yes, dear Eliza, though that would be the worst part. I'd like to solve a crime."

Eliza glared at him. "You *dare* try something like that?"

"Yes, Mistress. You don't have to worry. One man alone can hardly restore Daylight."

There were audible gasps from around the table. Eliza bent his hand back viciously and looked at his palm, leaving his wrist over the flame. He could barely keep from reacting, except by gripping the table so hard with his other hand that he heard it crack. Eliza grinned but didn't move his arm. "What *kind* of crime?" she hissed.

"It's a murder-mystery weekend at a hotel. They get some people to act out a killing and let the guests figure it out," he cried, struggling to keep still and sound almost normal.

She laughed and released him. "Oh, Sinjen. That's too funny. Of course you can go."

Made in the USA
Middletown, DE
27 July 2024

57907624R00156